# I NAMED MY BELLY FAT

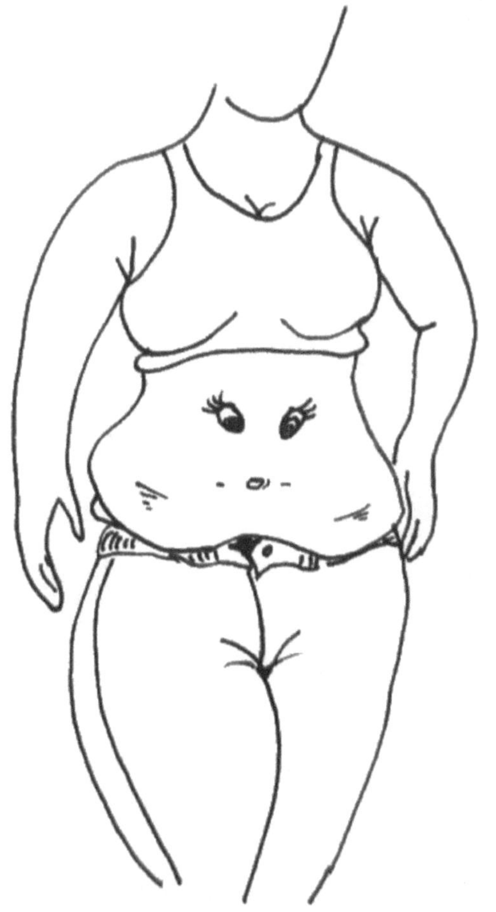

## CHARLENE

# BY LOUANNE MC FARLANE

When the narrator is dared to wear a bikini, it throws her into a tailspin. The demand to bare it all sparks more than wardrobe anxiety. It awakens a whole new personality.

Charlene, the belly fat that's been tagging along for years, shows up as a sassy sidekick in the journey towards self-acceptance.

This diary-style novel chronicles their hilarious and heartfelt struggles — one stretch mark at a time.

From passive-aggressive gym mirrors to the sacred ritual of unbuttoning jeans after dinner, *I Named My Belly Fat Charlene* is a love letter to every woman who's ever felt like her body was the punchline. It's not; it's the whole story.

# Contents

# FOR MY MOM

# One

## BEING FAT ISN'T FUNNY

*Thursday, November 9, 2017*

I think I need better friends.

Tanya has already left. Why am I still sitting at the coffee shop, watching muffin crumbs and feeling to cry into my half-drunk vanilla milkshake?

Just a half hour ago, we were laughing about Tamira's wedding jitters and wondering what color nail polish goes with mint green and chocolate. I was about to offer to write the toast she was dreading to make as the maid of honor when she dropped the bomb.

"That's enough wedding talk. It's still ages away, and that's all we talk about lately. You know my birthday is next month, so spotlight's on me. I've decided to do Bikinis and Martinis at the Neon Watering Hole!"

Bikinis and Martinis!!!

The Neon Watering Hole is a niche resort hotel with neon lights in the pool, crazy cocktail specials and usually a laid-back crowd of professionals. They host a wild karaoke session once a month at the swanky poolside bar. We never used to miss out on the fun. It was our happy place, but we haven't been for a while.

But does she mean I have to wear a bikini? Really? Me?

Let me add a little context, judgy journal, as to why I feel personally insulted by this theme. I have to give you some background. Tanya is not like me. She is not fat, at all. She's effortlessly slim and has always been super skinny and flat chested. In fact, she describes herself as a member of the "itty bitty titty committee". Tanya's idea of a hot outfit has always been some slashed-to-the-navel top or backless crop top, because her "girls" couldn't flash anyone. I would look obscene in any such style and have been called to HR for violating the dress code because I didn't button up my company polos. My "girls" are big women and they are in your face, all the time. Along with the boobs, I'm porting around a sizable tummy.

So, this theme, Bikinis and Martinis, feels offensive to me.

"Are we planning for sexy coverups too, and tankinis for the more generously proportioned?"

Tanya outright laughed at my suggestion.

"No. All the guests have to dress according to the theme, or it won't work."

I scowled at her and asked her point blank, "Do you really want my belly to attend this party?" She just hooted as if I had told the best joke ever. She also didn't answer me. Her phone buzzed and her attention was gone.

Tanya and I have always joked about our body issues as we tried to fit into fashion trends. While I try to erase or minimize my belly, she has always been trying to get more curves. She has put on some weight since we left college, but she's still svelte. She could still fit into those barely-there, short and snug bodycon dresses. I could only imagine wearing those with some TIGHT breath-snatching shapewear.

While she was texting, I gave the idea of me in a bikini some serious thought. I imagined myself, with my body, in a bikini, with my belly hanging out. I pictured myself standing around a trendy bar full of beautiful people with my whole belly outside. It got ugly in my mind, with the bartender scowling at me and the other girls elbowing me out of their way.

Then I imagined my belly fat as a whole personality, sharing my body with me, defending me. The idea was sitting on me, or in me, or maybe *with* me. I don't know, but it just started to make sense.

Before everyone became politically correct, there was a joke going around that said that inside every fat girl is a skinny bitch trying to get out. What if it was more like a split personality? Or like those werewolf/shifter novels where there's a whole other animal sharing the skin and spirit of the character?

I do have a fat appendage that has always been a part of me. I have always, always, always been self-conscious about my belly pooch and Tanya knows this. It feels like that body part has a mind of its own. I think she needs to be acknowledged. I've got to accept her. If I'm considering airing her out in a whole-ass bikini, I should give her a name, too.

"Well, Tanya, if I'm going to wear a bikini to your party, and put my whole body on show, I'm going to have to give my belly fat a name. I'll be introducing her to the world. I'm going to start calling her Charlene."

Tanya laughed until she got hiccups and had to drink some water. Then looked right at me and laughed some more. Finally, she asked me if I was joking. I sighed deeply, then smiled and shook my head.

"If I'm going to put her out there, I should respect her enough with a name. I'm going to have to make it official, too. Maybe even wear a name tag on my belly," I joked.

By then, Tanya wasn't even listening to me. She had gotten distracted by her phone again. She went back to it, chuckling to herself that I say the funniest things. Her concern for me was gone. Seconds later, so was she. Leaving me here wondering if my bestie had a lobotomy and didn't tell me.

Tanya, who's been my friend since we were assigned as college roommates, has heard me complain about my tummy for as long as she has known me. I was always a boobs and belly girl. In my smaller, glorious college days, I was probably a size 8 or 10. Still, I looked absolutely indecent in a tank top because of my D cups. Maybe the problem is she has heard me moaning about this for so long. I've used jokes to cover my secret shame for years. I shouldn't blame her if all she heard was "belly fat" and stopped listening.

But, I asked her outright, didn't I? She dismissed my feelings about her dress code and she was straight up laughing at the idea of me in her bikini party. I can't believe that skinny minx is laughing at me. AT me, not with me! I'm not laughing.

Why laugh about this? What's so funny? I was being serious. I *am* being serious.

I'm carrying around the weight of an extra person. If I'm honest, I'm probably at least forty pounds overweight. Okay, maybe seventy pounds, if you believe the BMI chart. If I followed that, I would need to be anorexic to get to their weight goal. I'm almost two hundred pounds, but a hundred and twenty pounds on a 5' 7" frame would be skeletal. If I'm carrying seventy pounds on my tummy, shouldn't I be able to name my fluffiness? That is a whole persona I've been struggling to control.

The way I figure it, a toddler weighs about thirty-five pounds. Charlene is almost twice the size of a toddler!!! She is bloated, gassy, and overly attached to me. Those are definitely toddler characteristics.

Still, Charlene is not just a joke, not just a reaction to her party idea. This wasn't a throwaway comment. This, Charlene, is a big deal to me. Charlene is such a big-ish part of who I am. She's been a huge part of how I define myself. I used to be a skinnier girl with a fat belly. Now I'm a fat girl with a fat belly. Charlene has been with me through thick and thin. She's been growing with me all along. I might as well get to name her if I'm taking her everywhere I go. When I go into a dressing room, my focus is making sure Charlene looks good. If Charlene is properly covered, only then do I feel good. I can't even imagine a scenario where I would be comfortable wearing a bikini in public. I have enough trouble choosing regular clothes.

I'm not into tent dresses, because who wants to look like a giant formless sack? I don't like tight clothes, because I don't like looking like a lumpy sausage squeezed into its casing. Miss me with the idea of flaunting a muffin top. Though, I actually like the term "muffin top". The top is the best part of the muffin anyway, so light and fluffy.

Charlene is no muffin top. She is a whole jumbo-sized carrot cake muffin. It might be those darned muffins from this coffee shop that helped her grow. But they have carrots in them; isn't that healthy?

I'm digressing. The point is, my best friend should already know my belly fat affects my self-esteem. She should have considered me in the party plans she knows I would absolutely support and cheer on. I'd be the one helping plan, decorate and set up. I'm the one in our friend group who gets the gang excited. I'm usually the life of the party. I've been helping her with all the maid of honor duties for her sister's wedding. Why would she shut me down for her birthday party?

What kind of bestie breezes off, leaving me sitting wondering if her party theme is deliberately exclusive? Does she even want me there? Am I overreacting?

If Charlene could talk, what would she say?

**Charlene:** *"Listen, there might be a neon pool and dirty martinis, but I'm the one bringing the curves and the cake to this party. I should definitely attend. I'd be the real guest of honor."*

*Friday, November 10, 2017*

It's been a whole day and despite all the coding issues I had today at work, I was totally preoccupied with Tanya's party. I am still in my feelings over naming Charlene. Instead of meeting the crew for happy hour, I'm home tonight. I've decided to bake a cake, to keep myself from calling her and shouting in frustration. The cake is in the oven now, judgy journal, and yes, it is red velvet. While we wait for my comfort cake, help me figure this out.

Am I just being self-absorbed or is Tanya trying to tell me something? What if I'm missing the plot? Should I be trying to challenge my theory of loving myself 'as is'? What if Charlene doesn't have to be with me? I can troubleshoot my belly fat problem and come up with some solutions. A quick fix might be how I dress, but the logical solution must include diet and exercise. I probably need to change my diet, though I don't eat too much fast or fried foods. I don't even drink a lot of soda. I cook and I even enjoy my vegetables. Zucchini bread and carrot muffins have to count there. Ice cream and cheesecake should get a special dietary pass. They're full of milk and eggs; isn't that supposed to be the basis of a great diet? I only splurge when I go out to eat, and that is only once every two months or so.

Okay, maybe I can do better. I've been researching diets and getting quite discouraged when they say to cut carbs. You have to understand. I love pizza and cheesy bread sticks. I especially love hot homemade bread, with butter and a slab of extra sharp cheddar. That gets us in the feels. With my love for carbs and fats, according to these dietitians, I shouldn't be surprised Charlene is there. She's always rising to the occasion, looking like a fresh loaf. All the diets I have seen say to cut carbs, especially bread and pasta, and a whole lot of others say no dairy. No bread? No cheese? No cake?

It would be like having to amputate an arm or leg to cut bread or cheese out of my diet. Even if I wanted to amputate Charlene, we're just too attached.

It's not only about the delicious taste of bread and cheese. I'm attached to memories of my mother baking on a weekend. I love the smell of fresh bread in the oven, the sight of butter melting to golden goodness on a fresh-cut slice, the happy feeling of my family sitting together enjoying fresh bread and cheese. That is my comfort food. When I don't know what I want to eat or cook, my default setting is bread and cheese. Clearly, I need comforting now too, as the lovely smell of chocolate is soothing my soul.

When food is tied so closely to family, to memories of love and warmth, it is hard to decide a diet is worth more. How do I separate the joy of food from the need to diet? *Do* I need to diet?

How do I delete Charlene if she requires the deletion of a family history of what and how I eat? Charlene is proof I have lived, laughed, and loved carbs, and the carbs loved me back. It's proof my mom loves me and keeps sending me fresh-baked coconut loaves. Sigh.

How do I get around to wearing a bikini because it's my bestie's birthday and we're just going to have some fun? Does accepting Charlene mean I should wear one anyways?

**Charlene:** *"Girl, there are so many people literally starving for love. You are well loved and I'm the proof. Forget the spreadsheet. Get a bikini, and let's go eat birthday cake."*

*Saturday, November 11, 2017*

Do I have a bikini body? I was checking myself out in my bathroom mirror, dressed in my sexiest underwear, imagining it as a pretty bikini, and I could swear there was snickering.

Does anyone else have a judgmental mirror? Where can I get a mirror that gives me less attitude? I was alone in the bathroom and yet the mood was pretty disapproving. Definitely need to change that mirror.

But could I actually do it, wear a bikini, I mean? I've never worn one in my whole life.

Charlene assured me, *"Every body is a bikini body. If it fits, you can wear it. Ignore that mocking mirror."*

I remember when I used to be skinny. At least, I look at pictures of myself when I was younger and think, *Wow, look how slim I was.* What I remember about those days is being constantly concerned my stomach wasn't flat enough. I had to suck it in for every photo. I made sure to show off my cleavage to draw eyes away from my midsection. I would hold my breath and hope for the best. Now, I am forty pounds heavier, with a gut that can't be sucked in. I look back and realize I didn't even appreciate my body when it was "good"!

I've been trying to tell myself lately, I better love the body I have now. Imagine if in ten more years I am looking back thinking, *Wow, I was much slimmer then. If only I was still that size....* The reality is, I don't love my body and I never did, not when I was a size 6 with a little tummy, and certainly not now as a size 16 with a definite stomach and love handles. I'm wondering if it isn't my body that needs to change. Maybe it's my mind. I have to figure out how to love myself, how to love Charlene now.

I watch other women larger than me wearing spandex, squeezing into not-so-skinny jeans with their muffin tops spilling over, and still strutting in three-inch heels. Oh yeah, they are wearing their fat proudly. Some of them even look fantastic. I would love to have their confidence. Meanwhile, maxi dresses are no longer my friend, as my belly bulge is now competing with my cleavage. I am here every day, shaking my head at my reflection when every outfit comes with a big belly overprint. My mirror definitely has a negative spirit. Maybe I can sage that away, smoke out the miserable gremlin.

Why can those fatties wear anything they want, and look sexy as hell? In the same outfit, I would feel uncomfortable and self-conscious. I want to be a sexy fatty, too!

I can almost hear Charlene berating me: *"Girl, sexy is an attitude and I've got it. Let me be your cheerleader and we can banish that negative Nellie in your mirror."*

The trouble is, I still remember when I used to be skinny and I want to go back there. The next time, this time, in my skinny body with my belly pouch, I want to believe my body is just right. Or maybe now, in my fat body with Charlene, I need to believe my body is *still* alright. How do I get to that?

**Charlene:** *"Stick with me and let me coach you into sexiness. Belly up."*

*Monday, November 13, 2017*

Some days at work are the worst. My coworker, Marcus, thinks he is funny but he isn't.

I thought he was my friend, since we've known each other from college, but with friends like that, I might need to find a new job in another state. We, along with the rest of the coding team, were in a conference room discussing the software upgrade that is coming up. As always, the pre-meeting discussion descended into a complaint session about budgets and where money could go instead of to replacing the carpet in the executive suite. I was voting for better chairs, but the guys wanted to upgrade the break room with a pinball machine. Priorities, please!

Honestly, it wouldn't take a big budget increase to get us some better chairs. They can clearly afford it since there are all those fancy ergonomic chairs in the conference rooms.

Meanwhile, we, the software engineers and computer techs, who are literally sitting at our desks for about 14 hours a day, are in the most horrible chairs. The squeak on Marcus's chair distracts me when I'm deep into debugging.

"At least my chair still has hydraulics in it," said Marcus. "Your fat ass has sunk your chair into the ground."

"Hey, that's not fair. It was already broken when I got assigned to this cubicle. This stupid chair has nothing to do with my weight at all," I replied sharply.

Yes, it's true I can't adjust my seat. It isn't because I've gotten heavier over the years, although I have. Marcus, the jerk, knew me when I was slimmer and likes to tease me about my good ole slim college days. He thinks the fat jokes are cool cause "we are buds" and buds rag on each other.

I don't remember agreeing I was his "bud". His "jokes" aren't even funny, either. Is he excluding me deliberately and being misogynistic because I'm the only woman on the team? Or, does he think it's okay being obnoxious to me personally, since we are "buds"?

Guys just use jokes as an excuse for being mean to each other and it truly sucks. If I retaliate, I'm a mean bitch. If I get offended, I'm being a girl. If I ignore it, they just keep ramping it up to see what will trip me out.

Today, I brought in donuts for the team meeting. We usually take turns bringing in snacks to share on Fridays, but I needed a sweet pick-me-up this morning. Marcus announced to the room, "Well, well, looks like the fatties are looking to add members to their squad." Everyone else laughed.

I glared at Marcus, but Charlene wanted me to call him out. *"Girl, I wouldn't waste any more donuts on those guys. Keep the cakes and the calories for those who love you, like me."*

Marcus drinks about three Cokes a day and yet he has remained as wiry as in our college days. He eats burgers and fries most days, washed down with his sodas. Forget veggies; he proudly declares he is a carnivore. My diet is much better than his, and yet *I'm* the fat one. He claims it's because he plays football and runs, but could it be down to genetics and metabolism? Does physical activity make such a big difference? I read that diet counts more than exercise, but the evidence seems to weigh on the other side.

His last contribution to Friday snacks was a case of soda. How are my donuts today worse than that? I don't even drink soda. He had nudged me then, saying I should thank him for looking out for my health, and sparing me the calories.

Truly, I need to ask for a new cubicle assignment. That would solve my Marcus problem and his fat jokes. I need to get away from these "friends" that are dragging down my morale. Even if I do end up sitting closer to Greg with the flatulence and personal space issue, I might get a better chair. I'll just need to bring in some Febreze to make my space breathable.

I hate open plan offices. I should seriously consider rolling one of these conference room chairs across to my cubicle. Or just move my setup to the conference room. Are there any cameras in this hallway? Maybe I can sneak it across. With a better chair and some noise-canceling headphones, I might be able to keep working with these "buds".

**Charlene:** *"I'd insist on a better chair and a corner office, girl. Get away from those 'buds'."*

*Tuesday, November 14, 2017*

Is everyone against me now? It's truly the ones closest to you that can get those barbs in deep. When you think they'll be there for you and defend you, they just don't.

The Dude and I are not on the same page.

My boyfriend, who likes to be called "The Dude", can be brutally honest, or wickedly funny depending on how much he likes you. Sometimes with me, he's both. More often, he's quiet and sweet, but not in the usual ways with compliments, flowers and chocolate. He sees what I need and gets it for me. Like the slow cooker he got me when I got "promoted" to the server team, and had to work longer hours. He wanted me to have a meal ready to eat when I got home. When I get home to the delicious smell of beef stew, I mentally thank him again.

We work in the same building, but not for the same company. He is a mechanical engineer and works as part of the elevator maintenance team. Basically, he's responsible for the elevators, escalators and electrical systems for the 40-floor skyscraper. We hardly see each other in the building. We used to meet up for lunch, but too often, maintenance emergencies would interrupt our standing lunch date. Sometimes, he would have to miss lunch, but he'd still drop off something for me and continue on to his tasks. I had a fixed lunch hour and couldn't wait to eat with him. Instead, he comes over to my place for dinner most weekdays, and sleeps over on the weekends.

We were sitting together on my couch and I was complaining about Marcus and his fat jokes. The Dude said, "Why get mad at Marcus if he's telling the truth? You have gotten chunky."

"You shouldn't be taking Marcus's side. You're supposed to be supporting me," I said.

"I *am* supporting you. That skinny dude has been trying to get into your pants since college. He's just ragging on you now because he regrets he didn't get through with you. He's getting mouthier hanging out with that creep Greg, too. I told you he wants to be more than your friend."

I was completely blown away. I couldn't decide whether to be mad because he agreed I'm fat or concerned he's clearly jealous of my friendship with Marcus. He must be feeling insecure.

The Dude, Marcus and I all went to college together. The Dude's crew was in engineering, and Marcus and I were in computer science. I thought he considered Marcus a friend as well. They play football together on Sundays ... well, sometimes. My dude claims he plays. I often hear how he pulled his hamstring in the first fifteen minutes and spent the rest of the time on the sideline drinking beers, all reported by Marcus. Maybe they have a guy rivalry going on and smack-talk each other because they're "buds" too.

I decided I was more upset about The Dude's comment about me being fat. I work with Marcus every day and deflect his mean comments too often. There is NO interest there.

"Marcus is not checking me and I am not getting chunky," I insisted.

"Of course, my tubby babe. Gosh, don't get mad. I love your body. You and I are on the same page. We both have a single barrel. More of each other to love," he joked. I wasn't soothed, but he kissed me on my head.

"Hey, I bought shrimp wontons for you, and Chinese food for dinner. You don't have to wonder about what to cook. There's also cheesecake for after dinner. You know, I have to feed you to make sure you still have something for me to hold onto."

To his credit, The Dude is always on point when it comes to food. He anticipates my hangry moods, and is already planning the next meal while we're still eating. He knows the way to my heart is through food. He's literally always feeding me. I've decided he must mean well.

Besides, he makes a good point: we are so alike. My dude is big and cuddly and his single barrel makes a great pillow when we're watching movies together on my couch. Love handles are nice things to have sometimes.

Charlene approves, because maybe he has a Charlie?

**Charlene**: *"Girl, I was ready to fight him with you. Then I heard cheesecake. He can't complain you're fat and bring cheesecake. Why are you still writing? There's cheesecake!"*

*Saturday, November 25, 2017*

Charlene and I had a major falling out today.

She and I went shopping for swimsuits. This was not about Tanya's birthday. The Dude and I were talking about going on a vacation cruise. Okay, okay. *Maybe* I may have also been trying to visualize the possibility of me fitting into a full-coverage bikini for Tanya's party. I thought I was up to it. I have even been trying to diet for ten whole days (no bread – so hard, no soda – easy), but I didn't give up cheese. I managed to lose a couple pounds, so I thought, *yeah, things are looking up*. However, I was wrong.

First off, all you see in the store windows are micro bikinis, not even potentially workable tankinis. There don't seem to be any full-coverage bathing suits. The bikinis are, like, high-hip Brazilian-cut bottoms and triangle tops that only just cover your nipples. It's like they took the fabric ends from everything else and decided to recycle them into bathing floss.

Charlene wasn't even fazed by that. Now even my belly fat has a sadistic streak. *"If Tanya wants us in a bikini, let's give her a full show. All eyes will be on me."*

I'm not ready to let Charlene all hang out. I try to be modest, considering how much my clothes need to cover between my boobs and my belly. I was rummaging in the back of the store where they would usually stash the types of bathing suit with full coverage, the ones meant for aunties and grannies. There weren't even full one-pieces, only these cut-out abominations. The salesgirls called them monokinis. These fabric scraps had the sides cut out and some even with the middle cut out ... the very area that needs coverage.

I finally found a tummy control, basic black one-piece with slimming rouching on the sales rack. One lonely garment that was the last of old stock. I was so relieved to find it, then equally so disappointed when I tried it in the dressing room. All I saw looking back at me in the mirror was a whale. Did the evil mirror spirit follow me to the mall? What did the tummy thing control, and what did the rouching slim? Not Charlene!

*"Why are you trying to cover me up? The whole point is to show me off. Get a bikini, babe! I want to be the star of the show."*

We didn't find anything we liked in that store. Charlene is urging me to embrace the exposure and show it all off, but I'm not there at all. This also means there's no way I am getting into a bikini for Tanya's party. Maybe there was a hidden message associated with those dirty martinis: Charlene (and I) are persona non grata. Tanya wasn't actually inviting me at all. She was telling me not to come.

As for the cruise idea, it feels like a mistake, too. Who wants to sit out by a pool tanning anyway; I could get skin cancer! I'm not so sure my dude is on board with the cruise idea. He grunted something noncommittal when I asked him what he thought about it.

I just felt we should do something fun and different. Our last vacation was almost two years ago, and we went to Las Vegas with a bunch of friends, including Marcus. It was absolutely fun bouncing from casino to casino. It was an awesome time, but I feel like it was more of crew trip rather than a "just us" trip.

Now that I reflect on it, my dude took a lot of photos with the Vegas showgirls. They were all over, promoting the revues, the casinos, the drinks, everything. He got pictures with at least five different girls. Does he want a slimmer, sexier partner? I have lots of photos with the whole crew, but there are just two pictures of us together. Both of those photos were from the Cirque du Soleil's Zumanity show. My dude got pulled on the stage. He had to pretend to gyrate on another woman, who also got pulled out of the crowd. After the show, we got complimentary photos from the event photographer for him being such a good sport.

I was the photographer for all the other times, since I was the one with the camera. I took tons of photos of him on request, including those with the showgirls. He took none of me, even the night I thought the leopard print maxi dress I was wearing was sexy. He seemed to love it too. I remember him trying to dive bomb my cleavage.

Hmm, are there showgirls on the cruise, too?

I'm going to find a vacation cabin in the mountains for us instead. Even five pounds lighter, I'm not in the body space for sexy dresses or bikinis. I'm also not in the headspace to compete with hot babes in any kind of swimsuit. We could be all cloaked up in parkas instead of anywhere warm requiring bikinis. That would suit me just fine. We can hold on to our mutual barrels in a nice, secluded cabin.

**Charlene**: *"Girl, I like the good food, and hot chocolate part, but why hide out in a cabin when you could do a hot tropical vacation? I want to go for a swim."*

*Friday, December 1, 2017*

I haven't spoken to Tanya in a couple of weeks. Should I call her? Should I even be the one to call her? It still feels like she owes me an apology.

Charlene has been in my head, egging me on. *"You need to confront her and find out what's going on. You don't even know what Tanya was thinking. Stop fretting and start texting."*

But I don't want to reach out only to get roped back into doing wedding planning or token shopping, or whatever else she needs help with. If she knows I'm upset, then she should be the one to reach out so we can resolve this. Surely Tanya knows.

Charlene pressed again: *"How's she going to know how you really feel if you keep joking about it, or worse, ignore even talking about it?"*

Charlene is right. I've been brushing it off, pretending it doesn't matter, but it does. I'm not going to help plan a party that feels designed to embarrass me. And maybe Tanya doesn't need my help with the wedding stuff, or her speech, or anything else.

I thought we were tighter than this. If she doesn't call me, then that says all I need to know.

**Charlene:** *"If she doesn't call, and even if she does, can we have lasagna?"*

*Sunday, December 10, 2017*

Well, it's official now. Charlene and I did not go to Tanya's party last night. For many, many reasons:

1. I'm still mad at her for insisting on a bikini theme and laughing about Charlene.

2. I didn't lose any weight and may have eaten my body weight in muffins this week alone.

3. I still don't own a bikini and would not be willing to wear one if I did.

4. The Dude also noted he was not invited, even though he knew it was a girls' event. He protested that if he can't hang with bikini babes, then neither should I. He was joking, but also not.

5. There has been a major backup server crash in my office and I pulled two sixteen-hour days getting it back up and running. I just want to sleep, eat and sleep some more.

6. Tanya also NEVER mentioned anything else about it since that day in the coffee shop about a month ago. I got the hint. I wasn't actually invited.

7. Actually, Tanya and I haven't even spoken since that day in the coffee shop – no phone calls, no email, not even a text message. It has been a month of radio silence.

Charlene is my best friend now.

**Charlene:** *"Girl, I have always been your bestie. I'm not going anywhere. Better get a bikini so The Dude can hang with a hot bikini babe right in your living room."*

*Two*

# Spanx and color diets don't compute

Tuesday, December 26, 2017

Charlene and I are agreed on one thing: Christmas calories do not count.

We are sprawled on the couch, after just returning home from my family's Boxing Day feast. I have to call it a feast. There was food for thirty people and there were only ten of us there. The takeaway boxes in my fridge will feed me for the next three days. I'm not complaining. I'm just not going to move for the next couple of hours while I invoke some snake digestion.

Christmas season lunches and family dinners are the epitome of love food. It is a true labor of love to cook so much food. Hours of baking ham and turkey, garnishing and setting them up, are deliberate messages of devotion. There's no way I am turning down handmade sweetbreads, cakes, pies and desserts. Who is the unhappy, bitter cretin that said not to drink calories?

Has that sad person ever enjoyed a spiced holiday eggnog? Yes, I meant spiced, not spiked, but I'd take the alcoholic version any day. It is protein, milk, and sugar and absolute joy (joy = rum) in a single drink. It is meant to be savored and indulged and absolutely enjoyed with no remorse.

My mother loved holiday cooking. She believed the smell of good food was a welcome to guests. She got up early and started before the family stirred. The whole of Christmas day consisted of eating to excess. Breakfast was served on the special china and it was as good as any fancy hotel brunch. Of course, lunch was a bit later, but it was not upstaged at all. Festive rice, cornbread, turkey, ham and sometimes stewed beef made an appearance. All that protein was followed by generous pies and sweets. The only way to manage was to stealthily unbutton the jeans and wear a long, flowy tunic so no one noticed. In fact, stretchy pants must be made for feasting occasions. You must leave room for the food.

Even Charlene had something to say about that. *"Have you noticed the best chefs are chunky? Good food requires a sacrifice of abs."*

The Dude agrees with me. Festive occasions call for food. Even better is the fact that he loves to cook and experiment with new recipes. The week before any of our family dinners, he tries out smaller portions to get the flavors right. I'm always ready to help him as the sous chef. It feels good to be working together in the kitchen and watch his eyes light up when I taste his handiwork and approve. He's been perfecting holiday fruit cake. He doesn't like the dense commercial versions, so he had been scouring recipes to improve it. He had me taste-testing his version, which I admit is lighter and fluffier. He claims it is a Caribbean version that has the best texture. With all the alcohol in the recipe, it must qualify as a rum cake, not a fruit cake.

He swears it's brandy, not rum. Either way, it is potent, but deliciously so.

The bottom line is, skinny jeans and I will not get along for the next month. Actually, who am I kidding? That fashion never got along with me. After this Christmas season, that wardrobe item has definitely veered into the no-go zone.

Charlene and I felt the love this season. We ate, savored and enjoyed the generous ministrations of The Dude. We're fully sated and I will probably wear some looser clothes for a bit.

We regret nothing.

**Charlene:** *"Yo ho ho, rum plus cake; those Caribbean pirates found the treasure."*

Friday, January 5, 2018

Ugh, January! The month of failed resolutions and short-lived hopes. It is also the month of reminders that I got sold a bridge to nowhere and got locked into an annual contract with the gym that I never go to. Around September last year, I felt guilty about the waste of money and I went in for a class schedule, but still never made it to the gym to actually work out. I know I should just cancel the subscription, but every January I swear I am serious now, and this new year will be different.

Well, it's January 5th and I still haven't made it to the gym. I can't keep getting suckered by this monthly payment. Do you know how many more lattes I could have bought with that membership?

"Why haven't you canceled the membership already, since you keep complaining about the charges?" The Dude asked.

"I tried. But the service desk told me there is a penalty charge because I signed up for a special annual subscription plan. There was some fine print clause about if I moved, then I could get a waiver. I have to call the corporate 800 number to request it," I said.

Seriously, this gym membership is harder to get out of than those tricky escape-room parties. You are not my friend if you get me stranded in a group of drunk strangers, who cannot even read the clues, much less figure out how to count in odd numbers to crack the code.

"One of the mechanics with us invests in about $200 worth of Muscle Milk and protein shakes every month to keep up with his gym gains. He says the hot trick is to go to the gym at midnight when the traffic is light and no one else is there hogging all the machines. We should try that. Is the gym open twenty-four hours?" he asked.

"Dude, I'm not sure it's open at all. I haven't been there in three months, cause it's on the other side of town. I'm only sure it still exists because I'm still getting billed. I'm in this apartment almost two years now, so I have had membership there for years," I said.

"Well, we should drive over there and we could upgrade to a group membership. Then we can go together and follow the shred plan Mike uses. I'll keep those gym bros from harassing you, and as a bonus, you could have a hunky boyfriend for the new year." He winked at me.

"Sure, we can," I said. That was sarcasm, dearest journal. Mentally, I was rolling my eyes at him. Yeah right, let's go shred at ten p.m. He falls asleep at eight. The TV remote is all cracked up because it is always falling out of his hand. When I check on him, the TV guide is on the screen watching him sleep. Who's he trying to kid? Is he getting up at ten p.m. to meet me at the gym for a workout?

I agreed with him rather than argue the point. I know his laziness is going to kick in and we are never going to get to the gym. In fact, I'd be surprised if he got there even to be added to the membership. I will just wait this enthusiasm out.

Oh wait, did he miss the whole part in the conversation where I said I was trying to CANCEL my gym membership? Guys just don't listen. That's why I can't send him anywhere to buy anything for me. He always gets sucked in by the salespeople and comes home with whatever the sample girl is peddling, and never gets what I wanted.

Do I look like I need freaking maternity pads? He blithely said the salesgirl promised that I would thank him for bringing a sample. Really??? I am not thankful. I'm insulted.

Do I LOOK pregnant!!! Well, actually... maybe I do. *sad face*

Charlene has tiger stripes (aka stretch marks) and I haven't even had one child yet. Sometimes I wish I were pregnant so it would be okay to have a big tummy. I have even shopped in the maternity section for stretchy pants, because they're just that much more comfortable. I have to dress the body I have, right? Charlene does not shrink for anyone else's comfort. She does not zip up quietly. I have a pair of jeans that won't go up anymore, even if I roll around on my bed. It might be those Christmas pounds hanging on for dear life.

**Charlene:** *"Girl, these stretch marks are battle scars. I fought those jeans and won."*

Saturday, January 6, 2018

Charlene and I are in crisis mode.

Tamira's wedding is in three weeks. Although, Tanya and I still aren't talking, I have to show up for her sister's wedding. I am invested, since I helped with so much of the pre-planning. I helped make a thousand butterfly bookmarks. I damn well need to see how those are featured in the place settings. Of course, since Tanya is a bridesmaid, I know she will be in full glam mode. I'm not trying to compete or upstage or anything. I know my role. She's the hot one, I'm the smart, funny one. Plus, it's the bride's day anyways. Nonetheless, I want to look amazing and I've been looking forward to this. The Dude and I don't do a lot of events that require dressing up.

So, Charlene and I need to get it together. I searched my wardrobe and I couldn't find anything that fits, and looks good without overemphasizing my cleavage, or worse, my belly.

I went into the dressing room of this pretty fancy-dress boutique today. I was on a mission. It was brightly lit and the red dress on the mannequin in their show window looked like it would caress my curves and make me look like a Marilyn Monroe-esque bombshell. I felt a slight surge of excitement. I was not just trying on clothes. I was trying on confidence, style, and self-expression, rolled into one amazing dress package.

A personal shopper came to assist me. She was so stylish, dressed in all black, wearing a pair of high-waisted pants and a long-sleeved mock turtleneck. Only naturally lean people can wear a whole lot of fabric and still look svelte.

Her first words to me were, "Oh, bestie, you're so pretty, but you just need to lose a little weight around the middle." I gritted my teeth at this fake bestie and said nothing, because again, I only wanted that draped red dress to look awesome on me.

"Everyone is asking about that piece. We have a lot of big sizes and lots of other plus-sized options, too. Let me pick out two other styles for you to try on, along with the red dress. Some of those cuts aren't so forgiving," she said.

Red flag!! When the plus sizes are still available, things aren't cute or they aren't plus-sized. Let's just say the dresses, even the plus-sized ones, and I didn't quite see eye-to-eye, or should I say, waist-to-zipper.

Indeed! How can something that's supposed to be my size fit so badly! It draped in places where it shouldn't, like my boobs. Was it cut to fit an anime queen with humongous melons and an incongruously flat stomach? It clung the most exactly where I didn't want it to, right over Charlene. Aargghhhh!!! I looked like a badly packed, sparkly sequined red sausage. It was not a good look.

The dress was clearly designed for someone with the metabolism of a hummingbird. Even if I flapped my arms a thousand times a minute, there would be no fat burning effect to shrink my midsection. I contorted my body into a human pretzel, but only got the dress wrapped around my neck. Are these clothes made only for literal mannequins? How is this even a size 18? Last I checked, real people come in all shapes and sizes. Am I the proud owner of the "unique and challenging" size 16 body?

I struggled with the fabric that seemed to have a vendetta against me. I was sweating so hard, it felt like a cardio workout. Even the second dress that my personal shopper "bestie" recommended didn't fit, either. I stepped into that one and it got stuck on my hips. I had to struggle and contort like a snake to take it back off. This must be some unusually cruel cosmic punishment for those cheesy breadsticks and that extra slice of pizza last night.

I walked out of the changing room and dispiritedly sifted through the racks of dresses in the back. My initial enthusiasm had turned into frustration. It was on my way out, I noticed the dress didn't even fit the mannequin! It was pinned up haphazardly in the back to make it look good. It's all a scam.

After losing the wrestling match with those unforgiving fabrics and dresses, I reasoned this wasn't even about fashion, or fitting into those dresses. It was about fitting into my own skin. I made the decision that it was time to break up with Charlene. I have to go back to my spreadsheet of options. I need to lose some weight before dress shopping again.

I'm not trying to conform to society's standards or to impress anyone at the dreaded wedding. I do have a very particular phobia about the photographer having to figure out how to pose everyone to hide the fat girl. I can't keep trying to suck in my belly. I used to love being in pictures, but now I hate seeing my own photos. My eyes always zero right in on that unforgiving blob.

*"What unforgiving blob? I'm very giving... I give curvaceous. Don't hide from the photographer. I want my close-up,"* Charlene insisted.

I want to feel good in my own body, and maybe find a dress that transcends time and space and reverts me to a size 10. Or find the magic compression shapewear that shrinks my midsection but doesn't make me feel constricted. When I try squeezing into Spanx, I find I need to go to the bathroom three times as often as normal. I swear it is nearly impossible to pull your Spanx on and off in a public restroom. I've tried and I was sounding like an injured rhinoceros. No one wants to hear grunting and wheezing in the stall next to them. Someone knocked on the door and asked me if I was alright. With my Spanx squeezing off circulation to my diaphragm, I could only just gasp out some reassuring phrases. I don't want to have to do that in the middle of the wedding after having three celebratory glasses of champagne.

How about I get some liposuction too, and some compression bandages before this wedding? *frown face*

**Charlene:** *"Girl, forget those compression tights. I'd recheck those size tags. It's a sizing conspiracy in the fashion industry. Pinning the dress on the mannequin is false advertising, too."*

Tuesday, January 9, 2018

I watched a video today about the life of a plus-sized model. She looked so beautiful, so happy, so free... so much like me, but beautiful even in her underwear.

Somehow her stretch marks didn't look like flaws. Her jiggly belly didn't seem as jiggly as mine. I didn't even notice her cellulite. I was mostly wondering where she shops to get outfits that make her look so fabulous in and out of her clothes. I get nervous just walking into a dress shop. I feel judged by the salesgirls, because I know they're assessing whether I should be trying on anything in there. I feel like the store is perpetrating fraud if something is labeled XL and it's still too tight on me.

Sometimes, my shame is too great. I will buy an outfit I took into the changing room just so the salesgirl doesn't whisper about me when I leave. Do they gossip about the customers, wondering how I squeezed myself into that dress?

SPANX – that's how! At least, that's what I usually tell myself. I imagine if I were wearing my Spanx it would zip up easily, too. Except there are at least three dresses with tags on in my closet waiting for that magic Spanx to erase some inches. It will either take me fitting into some Victorian-era corsets or for me to lose twenty pounds for those dresses to make their debut... whichever comes first.

I never go shopping with my Spanx on. First off, I like to breathe. Second, what would be my excuse if the clothes didn't fit? Then I would have to admit my belly is too big. I am at an awkward size where I am too big for the regular stores, but not big enough for the real plus-size stores. I am between a size 14 and 16, and that is truly no-woman's land. Too big for XL but not big enough for XXL. Those sizes are always the ones sold out first. Why don't stores cater to women who are in that uncomfortable size range?

Either way, I feel embarrassed when I walk into a store. The salesgirls size me up and quickly decide that I can't wear anything on their racks. Or else, they seem to think my mom jeans and tunic top aren't stylish enough to justify their help, or even their attention.

Actually, I hate when they give me too much attention. Like when they want to hang out in the changing room to see how it fits. I don't need you to judge how the dress clings to my belly. Or worse, if they suggest, "Maybe with some shapewear?" Don't lie to me, sneaky salesperson, and tell me it would look great if I got the proper undergarments.

I know in my head that if I have to wear Spanx with a dress to look good, then it just doesn't fit. Even if I pretend sometimes that the magic Spanx will delete my excess curves.

Charlene was not feeling sympathetic about my angst. *"How about you stop interpreting every look as a sneer. They're probably bored, waiting for anyone to buy something in their store, including you."*

Under the microscope of "helpful" salesgirls, I typically pick something that's a bit too big, just to not feel like my clothes are grabbing me, and shuffle away from those judgy eyes. Then my newly-purchased potato sacks get buried in the back of my closet until my period week, when I'm so bloated the extra fabric makes sense.

So, again, I was left wondering, where do the big girls shop? How did the plus-sized model make it look so easy and effortless? I was in awe of her and also annoyed by her breezy style. It was only at the end of the video I realized she was a size 8. Size 8!!! How is that plus-size? What does that leave for us size 14+ girls? What are we, jumbotrons?

Sigh. Charlene and I have a date with Häagen-Dazs tonight. That pint of ice cream fits us fine. If nothing else, she's there for me when nothing else seems to be sticking.

**Charlene:** *"Girl, you had me at ice cream. Nothing fits as good as delicious food tastes. Savor the moment."*

Thursday, January 11, 2018

I was desperate. My wedding weight loss plans haven't started, so I decided to do something drastic.

I tried some dumb color diet crap that I saw online. I should have thought this one through a little more. I mean, how many foods are orange? Anyway, I took an online test designed to identify my metabolic type and then I was supposed to eat the color food that corresponded. There were about twenty-five questions in the quiz, and it all seemed pretty logical and thoughtful to me. By the end, it concluded that my sluggish metabolism called for high energy orange food to jump-start my weight loss.

What a bunch of baloney. I ate pumpkin soup, cantaloupe, and carrot sticks, and drank orange juice for three days, and then fainted in the office. I opened my eyes to see Marcus hovering over me, and Greg saying that someone should unbutton my shirt. It was so embarrassing. Fortunately, most of the office was out on an offsite teambuilder. The three of us were supervising a server install and had to stay on premises, so I didn't have any other witnesses.

I was lucky that Marcus was my rescuer. I was also lucky I didn't start turning orange on that stupid diet. That happened to some people. Apparently, the orange pigment in those foods can accumulate in your skin and turn you literally orange. I didn't get to that point, because I just could not stand this diet. There are no orange proteins. Plus, I was always hungry and cranky.

I ended up literally starving and dehydrated. I was totally calorie- and vitamin deficient AND I lost no weight at all. I had an upset stomach for two out of those three days, and I was gassier and more bloated that ever before. Then the lack of actual food left me constipated.

Plus, I had some bad headaches from not having coffee for three days. I totally needed some caffeine, because there isn't any orange coffee out there anywhere. Needless to say, Charlene was also not amused. She's a fan of late-night snacks, and Cheetos weren't cutting it.

Who comes up with these diet ideas? Or rather, I should be saying who believes all the crap they see online? Me, that would be me. I'm the poor sap that fell for it. Desperate times might have called for desperate measures, but say no to the color diet.

Charlene definitely did not approve of that diet plan. *"Why am I being punished with a cantaloupe diet? Eat some real food, please!"*

The cheeseburger Marcus brought for me when I fainted in the office tasted damn good, though. Does a cheeseburger count as something orange, as the cheddar cheese is strangely orange? How about if I dye all my food orange? Would that wake up my metabolism?

I'll skip color dieting for a bit. I don't know that fad diets can be any kind of solution. I have to eat to live. I don't want to restrict myself so radically, even for a short time. I need to figure out a longer-term solution to my diet issues. In the meantime, real multicolored food for the win.

**Charlene:** *"Diet culture ignores reality. Girl, please let's just eat. Please."*

Friday, January 12, 2018

Marcus brought me lunch again today. Apparently, my fainting episode in the office worried him and now he thinks he needs to feed me to keep me healthy. He is being so considerate that he is making me rethink my judgment of him as a bad friend.

He actually apologized for the fat jokes, saying he didn't know I was getting an eating disorder. I protested that I don't have an eating disorder. He assured me, "You need to be eating more than rabbit food. You're not so fat that you need to go on a starvation diet. You could probably just come play football with me and the maintenance guys on weekends, and you'll be back to your college weight."

Running and sweating has never been my jam, nor is spending time with the maintenance guys. Besides the extreme body odor, their whole vocabulary is swear words.

"Tell Lucy she can take you to the cheesesteak sandwich place tomorrow instead of that salad place. She could try to get some meat on her bones, too. You need to eat to keep up with guys in coding," he said.

I usually get lunch with the office receptionist, Lucy. She's awesome and matches my energy when it comes to people watching and shit-talking. Plus, everyone is her friend, including the strangers who stand in line with us. I love her positivity, and besides, I need some female mojo since I'm surrounded by guys for all my working hours. She put me on to a salad buffet joint where we typically get lunch a few times a week. Marcus tried to invite himself along, but said the salads don't fill him up and he can't even understand what we are talking about.

Since The Dude's comments, I've been watching Marcus more closely. I don't know how The Dude had the wrong idea about him. Marcus knows that I have been with my boyfriend since my last year of college. The Dude and I worked together on an engineering project, and nights in the lab together turned into all our free time together. He kept hanging out with me and then introduced me to his parents as his girlfriend at his graduation. In my mind, we had been official months before. We never had to talk about our relationship. We just fit each other so well. Somehow, we found jobs in the same building and we have been going strong almost four years now.

Meanwhile, there has never been anything romantic between Marcus and me. Not back in college, when he barely spoke to me outside of classes, and not now working together for two years. Marcus has the cubicle right next to mine, so it's not like we don't still see each other and talk all day long.

"The other guys were ragging on me for buying you lunch. They say I'm your work husband. Don't get any ideas, though. It's because I keep telling Greg to lay off you. He's always checking you out. I told him you weren't into men who still lived with their mother," Marcus explained, looking embarrassed and uncomfortable.

"Anyways, I need you around, since you're the best coder here and you cover me when that dickwad James tries to shut down my compilers. He doesn't even know you wrote those scripts to restrict his access. If you die on me, it will be a cutthroat scene in here. You keep everything running. The guys are all secretly in lust with you and I'm the only one holding them off from hitting on you constantly. Greg said he dreams of laying his head on your breasts."

When he said that last part, I knew he was just messing with me to make me laugh. The other tech guys do talk about women all day long. They're completely inappropriate most of the time, and yet they have never been rude, suggestive or offensive to me directly. It's true that Greg has given me some creepy looks. But how do I report to HR that I don't like how a coworker looks at me? Not one of them have asked me to do anything more than join the group for happy hour – which I do on rare occasions. Only if The Dude meets us there, I'll go drink a few beers and leave before anyone gets too crazy. I don't believe any of those guys look at me as anything more than a coworker. Still, it's nice that he was worried, and that he knows I'm the smartest one on the team.

Lucy came by to check on me for lunch but found me munching on the chicken fingers and fries with honey mustard sauce that Marcus brought. Charlene and I are on board with that, and it's almost orange, too. Since Marcus is feeding me and keeping the other guys at bay, I will keep him on the friend list for now.

**Charlene:** *"Girl, he brought us burgers! He and Greg are absolutely lusting over us. Why are you denying my appeal?"*

Saturday, January 20, 2018

I decided to try a less drastic diet thing: change more meals to a salad. I already do that salad buffet with Lucy where I pick some stuff and they mix it into a tasty bowl for me. I enjoy their salads, so I could do that home for myself. How hard could that be?

Well, it was way hard. My leap into the world of salads has been quite surprising. I didn't expect that a bowl of leaves could be so intimidating. At the grocery, I stood in the produce section, trying to figure out the difference between kale and spinach. Seriously, they both looked the same to me. I felt like I was on some sort of culinary expedition. I needed a seasoned explorer, like David Attenborough, to narrate my journey figuring out what would taste good in my salad bowl. Nothing looked like the mixed greens I had at Salata. Instead, there were about ten different kinds of lettuce and they all seemed to be more expensive than a bag of rice. I already know lettuce doesn't taste as good as shrimp fried rice, but I was determined to give a good showing.

I grabbed some other exotic sounding veggies that I could barely pronounce and headed home. What even are bok choy and quinoa? I hadn't had those before, but I needed more bulk to convert a lunch salad into dinner. When I was ready to assemble my salad supremacy masterpiece and conquer the world of healthy eating, my counter looked like the contestants' grabbings on a cooking show. Would I impress the judges and my tastebuds with my desperate chopping skills? Probably not.

I took my first bite of my ambitious salad, consisting of crusted almonds, kale, quinoa, croutons, cherry tomatoes and beet, and immediately tasted regret. Turns out, dousing a salad in creamy French ranch dressing doesn't automatically make it delicious. The whole thing just tasted soggy, and not the epitome of health.

Charlene sighed. *"From cantaloupe to croutons, this doesn't feel like a step up. I thought food meant love. Do you even love yourself?"*

I sat there, slogging through my sad sloppy salad, munching on almonds and slurping on kale, while The Dude chuckled at me eating "wet rabbit food". He was loudly enjoying a cheeseburger, smacking his lips excessively. I got his point. His lunch was delicious.

"That looks like it was put together by a toddler who thinks salad dressing is white ketchup," The Dude said.

"Not helpful," I retorted.

"You can have some of my fries, babes. You're looking hungry." He laughed, and shoved the fries closer to me.

I tried to remind myself that this diet journey was more than just shedding pounds. It's about being healthy, and maybe fitting into a bikini. I'm supposed to be discovering the joy of self-care and self-love. I'm aiming to uncover some abs beneath the layers of pizza and ice cream that Charlene has wrapped around herself.

What was worse was that not even twenty minutes later, after finishing my salad, I was still hungry. This was even after I stole about half The Dude's fries to get some salt in my bowl. I put a generous number of almonds in the salad to get the protein they said I needed to feel full. When does that start to happen? Because I am EMPTY!

**Charlene:** *"Girl, we deserve better than lettuce and kale. I don't just want fries. I want a burger, too!"*

Wednesday, January 24, 2018

I might be the problem.

Lucy and I were having lunch today and she innocently asked, "Where's your friend Tanya, the science writer? How come she hasn't come around recently? Did she finish the service manual she was moaning about the last time? What kind of machine was it?"

I couldn't answer about the service manual project. We hadn't discussed her work much lately, since our conversations for the past two months had been so focused on wedding planning details. Instead, I brought Lucy up to speed on our more recent drama and lack of communication. I launched into the whole saga about the bikini party, and Tanya being generally unavailable and ghosting me since.

"Oh, she must be drowning with all the demands her sister wanted for the wedding if you aren't helping anymore. And she has to find time to practice for her solo at the dance class revue, as well. I wouldn't worry that she's ghosting you. She had a lot going on besides work. Her life is not all about you, you know. Don't you remember she mentioned that the tap and modern dance class was getting recruited for parade events? I think she talked about auditioning the last time we met up."

"What tap class?" I asked, wondering how Lucy knows more about my bestie's schedule than me.

"She invited you to try out the tap class with her and you launched into some discussion about tap shoes, and not ever finding big sizes. She said it would be fun for y'all to do something other than go out to drink and eat. I texted her asking when the revue was so we could show up to support. It turned out I have an art museum showing with Michael. I hope she's enjoying it, and that tap was as easy to pick up as she'd expected."

I don't even remember the dance class conversation. Lucy shook her head disapprovingly.

"You're such a big personality, and you get caught up in your head, you know. You think everything is a program to decode. I'm sure you don't mean to dominate the conversation so much. Tanya barely gets a chance to talk about anything. Maybe she wanted her birthday party to be about her and not about you."

My heart sank. I thought I was Tanya's biggest cheerleader. Could she be thinking all along that I don't care about her, her feelings and her interests?

I've been nursing hurt feelings about her party and she might have a valid reason to be mad at me. I didn't even think about that. Maybe we can have a real girls' talk after the wedding and clear the air. The wedding is next weekend and we'll definitely see each other then.

Charlene wanted to be front and center, and confrontational as usual.

**Charlene:** *"Why wait? Go get a muffin, and then call your friend and find out what's going on."*

Sunday, February 4, 2018

Tamira's wedding yesterday was beautiful. The venue was a lovely park in the city, which featured a pedestrian bridge over a series of water features. The bride was gorgeous in a lace halter mini-dress. Her butterfly fascinator was unique but tasteful and the sparkly butterflies in her bouquet caught the light. I loved how the butterfly theme was carried through, and sighed happily to see that my handiwork looked so artistic.

Tanya was looking stunning in her calf-length mint green slip dress. Charlene and I wore a black potato sack. I mean, a basic boatneck knee-length black dress, nothing too exciting. The top didn't show any cleavage, though there was some sheer paneling at the chest and knee level. It was supposed to be elegant and slimming, with "intriguing lace detailing".

Tanya confronted me in the reception bathroom just after the food was served. She didn't even say hello before she started in on me. I think she was already drunk.

"You might be happy to know my party flopped. I didn't mean for you to take it so personally. You weren't there and still everyone was talking about you. They kept asking when you would show up. Jules and Sandy left early, and joked that your energy was missing. Everywhere you go, people look at your boobs and laugh at your jokes. I didn't want your breasts to steal the spotlight. Nobody even sees me. I'm just your skinny sidekick. I wanted everyone to see *me* at my party."

"Tanya, how much did you drink today? You're the hot one. I might tell a few jokes, but who's coming out to see the fat chick at a bar?" I asked.

"If I'm so hot and sexy, how come I'm the single one? You've had The Dude hanging on to you since college. Every time we go to the Neon spot, you have guys hanging around and I'm the third wheel," she slurred.

Good god! I've been thinking I'm the fat friend, her wing-woman, and she believed *she* was the sidekick. Clearly, we have been writing conflicting soap operas in our heads. I'm struggling to look as good as she does, and she thinks I'm stealing her spotlight. It's like we are fighting the same battle on different sides. Still, that didn't quite get her in the clear.

Apparently the eight glasses of champagne she'd had was serving as her truth serum. "I know I should have called you. Tamira wanted you at her bachelorette. But I told her you and The Dude were together... always on the couch. You know, you already have a boyfriend. I need to be the fabulous one so I can get a guy. I'm the only one here with no plus-one," she said.

"You're in the wedding party. You have a groomsman to pair with," I said.

"He has a girlfriend. He didn't even want me to hold his elbow to walk up the aisle. At, least you covered up, and you're looking ordinary tonight. Thanks for not upstaging me with all your cleavage."

Tanya had been worried I would upstage her at her sister's wedding? She was so very sloshed that I was feeling genuinely sorry for my beautiful friend. She didn't realize that she was the hot sexy one between us. I was watching our reflections in the mirror, and wishing we could switch bodies. Also, why didn't my black silk dress look "elegant and effortlessly classy"? I wasn't trying to upstage anyone, but I definitely wasn't aiming for "plain and ordinary".

Do all mirrors lie to us? Tanya's isn't uplifting her either. I was feeling bad for Tanya, but I was taking some real hits from her honesty, too. She was saying all her quiet thoughts out loud.

We hugged but I was feeling really conflicted about the whole scene. I'm not mad at Tanya anymore, but I wasn't feeling exactly warm toward her either. This was not the happy wedding festivity I had hoped for.

I left Tanya in the bathroom and asked The Dude if we could leave early. He was on board, because the wedding had a small plate tasting menu and he was still hungry. He claimed he needed more protein so he could work on his gains. We left and beelined for a burger joint instead.

When I checked my phone as we got back to my place, I saw that Tanya had called and left me a voicemail, too. I hate listening to voicemails and this one was a doozy. She called me from the wedding, babbling about how much she loves me and we are still besties. She said she didn't mean to make me leave the wedding. She wants us to sing karaoke together again.

I shouldn't be so judgy. I've also been drunk and said the wrong things to the wrong person. Still, her drunkenness revealed all her real thoughts to me. It wasn't about dance classes and me talking over her. She thinks I steal the spotlight and I play up my breasts too much.

I grumpily and ungraciously thought that, even without me around, she clearly hadn't found any guys at the wedding either, if she had all this time to leave me long voicemail messages.

I'm going to need to work on my glow up. If I'm not going to shape up, I'll need to dress up. Maybe it is time to look up a wardrobe consultant to help style me and cover my boobs and Charlene.

**Charlene:** *"Girl, Tanya was drunk and jealous. I wouldn't be taking any style advice from her right now."*

## Three

# HOW DO SKINNY PEOPLE STAY SO SKINNY? IT MIGHT BE PHOTOSHOP.

*Wednesday, February 14, 2018*

The Dude is not much of a romantic. He was always more practical, charming me with small useful tokens when we were getting to know each other in college. He would forget birthdays and anniversaries, but then he would randomly show up with a new fancy pen set the day after I remarked how I like fountain pens. So, I'm never expecting much on these commercial holidays. All the same, I was not impressed by his Valentine's choice, either.

The Dude's idea of a good time is an all-you-can-eat buffet, so his idea for our Valentine's dinner out was the friendly neighborhood Chinese buffet, where we eat all the time. He was so weirdly proud of himself for remembering to take me out.

"They advertised a two-for-one special for Valentine's", he shared. Our night out was a great deal to him. *sad face *

Now, I could write sonnets about good food and how it describes love and all that. Didn't I already write you a thesis about holiday cooking? Charlene and I value good food, especially home-cooked food. Both The Dude and I are fairly decent cooks, too. He even gets into extravagant tasting menus when he's inspired. Thus, when we go out to eat, it has to be absolutely worth the effort. I usually get all dressed up, and even put on makeup. I fit Charlene into something appropriately attractive, but loose enough that I can enjoy eating. The worst is when you're so squeezed into an outfit that you can't even think about food or you risk bursting some seams. Even breathing is a risk in the Spanx category.

A dinner out, and more specifically, a Valentine's dinner out, demands a certain reverence for the food and the occasion. An all-you-can eat buffet, sadly, is the antithesis of that. This is mass-market, slam-dunk food. This is the opposite of food made with love. The entrees here are made to be shoveled down and satisfy hunger. It may even be designed to deter healthy appetites in order to improve the restaurant's bottom line. This is nothing more than a nod to gluttony.

As for the food specifically, there may be one or two dishes that are really tasty. The rest is just plate filler. I couldn't think of a buffet restaurant that made me think, "*Oh yes, this is the real deal*". It has all been penny-pinching, basic food. I was not impressed by this choice.

I imagine I'm a low-maintenance girlfriend. We are both fairly laid-back, but this seemed especially low-effort to me. It just felt like he wasn't trying to impress, like he doesn't have to do anything to please me anymore.

Am I being mean? Okay. I could be generous. Let me try to put a rosy spin on this evening's outing. The location did have all the elements of a romantic restaurant. There was dim mood lighting at the tables and bright lights around the food serving stations. Each booth had the obligatory plastic flowers, and we were shown to the table with a single stemmed rose. It wasn't even dusty today. When the server offered, I opted for pink lemonade to imagine it could be a Moscato, even if served in a scuffed plastic cup. The Dude offered to help me carry my dessert plate; such a ladies' gentleman. Sadly, the chocolate square was especially dry and uninviting this evening. I opted for the self-serve yogurt with hot fudge chocolate syrup to round out the meal. I never have the maraschino cherries, though. I have a healthy fear of red dye #6. I can't remember where I learned that that's supposed to be bad for you. Oh wait, there was also the complimentary mint chocolate sweet we received while paying the bill by the door.

Let me rate this night out:

Company – 8/10
Food – 4/10
Ambiance – 3/10
Overall – 5/10

**Charlene:** *"I'd give an A for effort, but the food was not worth a jeans' unbuttoning."*

*Thursday, February 15, 2018*

How can I be a better friend? I have said that Charlene is my bestie, but I've been missing my gabfests with Tanya.

She'd been on my mind yesterday, so I sent her a late Galentine's message this morning. You know, one of those "celebrate and love yourself" type of things. I remember how down she was at the wedding about being single. I especially feel guilty, considering I have been complaining about The Dude's low-effort Valentine's, but at least I wasn't alone. I don't even know what Tanya did, or if she had a new beau or a date. We've shared a few texts about work and schedules, but haven't really talked since the wedding incident.

Lucy's words had some time to sink in as well. *Have* our conversations been one-sided? I have been so inconsiderate. Why haven't I been celebrating Tanya and encouraging whatever she's been up to? Between work, dance classes and her sister's wedding, she had a lot of stuff going on.

When I was in my feelings about Charlene, she was in hers about not having a plus-one. Being a bridesmaid put a spotlight on her. She's more of a girly girl than I am, but she also is quieter than me. I used to be the one to get conversations started, so I imagined that the idea of having to speak up for the toast might have been stressing her out, too.

She hasn't responded yet. I'm still hoping she will see that I can be the bigger person. Literally, but also, I may have been a bit ridiculous about her party. She shouldn't feel bad for not managing my feelings.

Charlene tried to give me a pep-talk. *"Girl, you can be the bigger person and still demand respect from your friends. Next time, we will show up at that bikini party."*

I would never have imagined Tanya would feel insecure about me, because I am insecure myself. We shouldn't even compare ourselves. There is no competition here. I want my bestie to be her best self, and I want to believe she wants the same for me. I don't want to ever feel like I am dragging her down.

Anyways, I'm not holding a grudge. I just wanted her to know that we're cool.

**Charlene:** *"Okay, Tanya has her own issues. If she ate some more pizza with us, it might help."*

*Saturday, February 17, 2018*

Tanya called me back.

She has been having the best time at her dance classes, and now wants to take her dancing to another level by trying out for a semi-professional dance troupe that performs at parades and events.

Now, Tanya and I are science-minded. She's working as a science writer in a medical equipment manufacturing firm. While I'm your typical girl nerd, chubby and into videogames and not many physical activities, Tanya meets none of the smart girl stereotypes. She's athletic and she loves to dance. In fact, she could be a nerd's poster girl, smart and sexy. She's a beautiful girl. She is of mixed parentage, with a white father and a black mother. Her short, curly hair is currently dyed red and although we're the same height, she always seems taller than me. She complains about her boyish figure, but except for the boobs, she is body goals to me.

Back to the topic, though. She needed portfolio photos for her application to the dance troupe. Of course, she asked me to take them, as I always have my camera ready. It is a bit of stretch to call me a photographer. I usually take photos of scenery on vacation, but hardly shoot people, though. So I figured it would be some good practice for portrait shots.

We met at her apartment's community pool. She was dressed in some short shorts and a bra top that almost gave her cleavage. We were poolside and the light seemed perfect. I asked her to pose and was surprised to see her doing handstands, headstands and all that craziness. I didn't even know she could do all that, or that she needed those kinds of shots. She insisted that she needed to show off her strength and flexibility in the photos. Do you have to be an acrobat and a gymnast to dance now?

That got Charlene thinking. *"When is my photoshoot? Where's my bikini? It's time for me to show off in a pool. Let's show them how the curvy girls do it."*

While she was flexing, I spent half the time trying to get the camera to stop blowing out the image and keep her in focus as she flipped around. I know enough not to take pictures of my thumb, but I do keep the camera set on automatic. It's a top-of-the-line DSLR, so it is a smart camera and takes awesome photos. While I was wondering what I was doing wrong, I was also trying to figure out, how the hell does she stay so skinny? She eats more than me and she eats all the time. Mother Nature is not fair at all.

We went to lunch after our little photoshoot. I opted for a chicken Caesar salad and Tanya had a cheeseburger and fries. I still feel like I gained two pounds and she probably lost an inch from all those handstands. It's just like that. The smell of food jiggles my fat cells and she can wolf the world down and still see abs. What is up with that?

**Charlene**: *"Forget Tanya's abs. We have our own appeal... curve appeal!"*

Sunday, February 18, 2018

Were we looking at the same pictures?

Yesterday, Tanya and I sat down to review her shots, and I thought she looked hot as hell. Maybe I missed my calling as a photographer. Or maybe it's the model that makes the photographer look like an artist. She even switched into a red string bikini mid-shoot and suddenly, it was a perfect bikini babe photoshoot. At one point, she half slid into the pool, doing a leg stretch using the handrail at the pool stairs. I was so impressed with her body, flexibility, and confidence. Every image looked stunning to me.

Meanwhile, Tanya shook her head the whole time.

"You need to Photoshop my arms," she insisted.

Her arms! If anything, I thought maybe her girls could use a little boost, but honestly, I hadn't planned on photoshopping anything.

To her, the hair on her arms ruined the shots.

"Tanya, you look amazing. No one else is looking at your arm hair. But to satisfy you, I'll do some light skin smoothing. Keep in mind, these are application shots. The interviewers will see you in person," I said.

"I wax my knuckles, you know. I'm so hairy and body hair grosses me out. I didn't think the camera would catch it, but in these ones where I'm wet, it's so obvious. Once I start making some real money, I'm going to laser off all the hair on my body, starting with my arms," Tanya said.

Really?!? Do people do that? And how much would that even cost? I'd never even noticed the hair on her hands. I guess I'm lucky, as my body hair is pretty sparse. I shave my legs once a week, but I've never thought about my arm hair. Do guys pay attention to that?

"Before the interview, I'll use some depilatory cream on my arms too," said Tanya.

I tried that once on my leg hairs. The smell was so bad it lingered for two days. I had to stay inside for the whole weekend to let it wear off. This is why I shave. I don't need to smell bad and repel anyone.

**Charlene:** *"Girl, if stinky cream is the price of smooth arms, keep the fuzz; no need to add fumes."*

Thursday, February 22, 2018

Is there a rule that skinny people should only date skinny people?

Tanya and I met this super cool guy in the coffee shop the other day. Troy was your average guy, not fat, not short but not super tall. He was dressed in a light-blue polo and khakis, with brown loafers. He had well-groomed hair, clean fingernails and he had manners. He made small talk with me, the "less attractive" friend, when she went to collect her toasted bagel and cheese order. To me, he seemed down to earth, and genuinely nice. Well, as much as you can tell niceness in ten minutes of casual conversation.

If I wasn't already hooked up with The Dude and also completely off his radar, I would give him a chance just for good hygiene and manners alone. Those things aren't as common as one would hope, especially with guys.

Tanya is harder to please. He gave her his number, and after he left I asked her if she was going to call him. She flatly dismissed the idea, saying,

"No, he's too fat for me. He already has the beginnings of a beer belly. I'm not into the dad bod."

I hadn't expected she'd be such a body snob. Though to be honest, I'm not surprised. I'm still in my feelings about how she laughed about me naming Charlene. We haven't talked about it since. However, like a glutton for punishment, I asked her what she thought of me and my dude, since Troy was too fat for her.

"The two of you are like an old married couple, you fit each other so well. I think it's so cute, like a pair of roly-poly panda bears."

I didn't know if to be offended or complimented. I like the idea of being a panda bear. They are adorable and prized animals. But she's calling me and The Dude *roly-poly* bears!

Charlene piped up. *"It's absolutely a compliment. Everyone loves soft, cuddly pandas. You are a treasure and giver of awesome hugs. Soak up that love."*

That's why I decided today would be another salad day, since I'm clearly too tubby in the middle to be her friend. Once again, if I am being honest, it's usually a salad day for me when I'm hanging with her. I wonder if I subconsciously feel more overweight than usual around her. Why am I always feeling subtly insulted by her when we hang out together? At the wedding, she said she was jealous of my curves, but she never seems particularly complimentary about them.

Maybe it isn't what she says, but how that makes me feel. It's not her, it's me... no – it's her. Didn't I say I needed better friends? Maybe I need to be a better friend to myself?

**Charlene:** *"Hey, I'm your best friend and I like dad bods, and burgers. Maybe you need to stop joking about weight with Tanya and tell her how you really feel."*

*Friday, February 23, 2018*

If I had a magic debugger to diagnose and fix all my body issues, would Charlene be the only change I'd make? I feel like I'm hyper-fixated on my belly. Perhaps Charlene isn't the problem at all. Would I change my focus onto something else?

Here's what would be on my list:

- Face and body moles. I usually cover the obvious ones with my concealer.

- Eyelashes. I haven't tried extensions, but I'd like my eyelashes to be longer – that's why there's mascara. I'm not born with it.

- My hair. I'm okay with my body hair, but my hair could be longer and curlier, or maybe actually not curly at all, just wavy.

- Oh wait – chin hairs! I would absolutely get rid of chin hairs, along with the pesky, too-dark hair over my lips. Sometimes, it looks like I have sideburns. Okay, so all facial hair besides eyebrows and eyelashes has to go.

- Colored contacts. I tried colored contact lenses while I was in college, too. But it's such a pain always having to clean and maintain contacts. Plus, after a few hours, my eyes were irritated. So, I've changed my mind. Forget contacts of any sort.

I guess I do have a full list of things I might change. I would have said that I love myself just as I am, but somehow it doesn't seem so after all. I'll draft a spreadsheet and see what my options are, and work out a plan to solve some of my real issues.

**Charlene:** *"Girl, you don't need to change a thing. You're fabulous, as is. Are you still comparing yourself to Tanya?"*

# *Four*

## APPARENTLY, YOU CAN'T BE SKINNY ENOUGH



*Sunday, February 25, 2018*

There is no logic in the world today, or maybe there is totally just some real karma out there.

Tanya went with our awesome super-filtered photos to her dance interview and came back broken hearted. The dance troupe leader declared she was too thick to be in the troupe. Man, I swear she is the definition of a stick. She has a decent-sized butt, so maybe she isn't an "I" but a "b" shape. Anyways, that is the only part of her body that has any fat at all. The maintenance guys informed me that if a girl has no breasts, she should at least have some ass. Then they complimented me on my rack and asked if I needed help holding them up. (Ugh, NO!) This whole conversation occurred while they were delivering my new ergonomic chair. Marcus was not around to keep the comments in check, so it turns out he may have been my white knight after all. While I may have the boobage and some of the butt the guys seem to like, my assets come with a large side of belly, too.

Meanwhile, Tanya, the beautifully slender sweet gal, was told she needs to work out, slim down and then try again. I was like WHAT... jaw-to-the-floor thing. She was totally freaked out. Now she's planning to start working out in beast mode to try to fit their imaginary standards. I mean, how slim do you have to be to dance?

From our awesome photos, it's clear she's already limber and flexible. Maybe it was female insecurities or hormones or something on the part of the director, because my friend is cute and hot. I hate for it to be an evil woman feud, but I don't think her weight or size is the real issue.

I was telling her not to take this so personally, but she is already talking about how she is going to be my personal trainer, too. She went off on how we should be accountability buddies. Suddenly, I am part of the weight loss party. Wait, don't sign me up. I'm sure I told her naming Charlene was about accepting my body. When did I say I want to work anything off? My idea of working things out is a Swedish massage. How did she turn her issues back into a conversation about my body?

I was thinking, *honey, have some ice cream and waffles and then if you like to dance, we can dance it off with some Zumba or something.* This thinking here may account for my lack of abs. I want Charlene and me to get into a chill place, a Zen zone of calm acceptance. I don't want this gym thing to throw us off balance.

Can I be a supportive friend and still not go to the gym with her? I mean, she doesn't even need to work out. She doesn't have, like, rock definition abs, but I can see her ribs. She could be just one skipped meal away from an eating disorder, if you look at her. But I see how she eats, and unless she hides to chuck, it's unlikely she has an eating disorder. To my mind, if you can already see ribs, losing more weight is going down the crazy rabbit hole.

I can't see my ribs, but should I be able to do so? Shouldn't seeing your ribs be the definition of "you are totally slim enough" for anything?

I don't think I need to go to the gym, anyways. I know I'm not skinny, but I'm healthy enough. I am not obese. I am not saying this to convince myself. Yes, I have seen my BMI numbers, but weren't those based on European soldiers or something? That's an outdated algorithm. This is the modern era where dress and body sizes have clearly changed. Shouldn't the BMI number chart move to suit?

**Charlene:** *"Girl, forget Body Mass Index; those numbers were for soldiers. I'm a general and you can count on me for Belly Motivation and Inspiration."*

*Monday, February 26, 2018*

When I told Marcus that Tanya tried to sign up for a dance troupe and got turned down because she wasn't skinny enough, he leaned back in his squeaky chair and stared off into space.

"What, are you zoning out on me?"

He turned and grinned. "I was just remembering Tanya. She was pretty cool in college, but she had no breasts. Did she get fat or something?"

I shook my head at him again. "Really, you are asking me that question? Is that all you can focus on? My whole point is she isn't fat at all, and they told her she needs to lose weight. I swear she looks just like when we were in college."

"Yeah, that's what's wrong with the world," Marcus declared. "Too many women are trying not to look like women, trying to be super skinny and have no curves at all. Does she want to look like a bodybuilder, then?"

"When did you get so obnoxious about women? I seem to remember you as being much more respectful. You're spending too much time with that perv Greg."

I reminded him that Tanya wasn't the one who wanted to be thinner. It was the dance troupe director who thought she wasn't lean enough.

He agreed that getting skinnier would not be a good look for her, but for completely different reasons. He insisted that a woman should have curves, not muscles. Women could work out but not overdo it. I rolled my eyes at him. Why does he get to dictate how women should look? He was warming up to his fat spiel and I was ready to tune him out. He can be so shallow and condescending.

"If women are supposed to be so fit and slim, what about you guys?" I challenged him. He dared to tell me he is totally fit. Just to be clear, Marcus does not go to the gym, but he said "his woman" would need to exercise because she needs to look good and stay healthy. Since he plays football weekly, he claimed he is doing his part to stay healthy for his woman.

"What woman are you talking about, Marcus? Aren't you single?" I retorted because his macho talk was beginning to irritate me.

"I'm not... yeah, not single. There's someone I'm talking to..." he stuttered.

"That's not what we're talking about anyways. Don't get mad at me because I'm not interested in going out with you. We're just friends. If we were a couple, I'd encourage you to work out with me," he said.

"As your friend, I'm telling you, you need to slim down a bit, and maybe dress a little nicer. You ladies like to tell guys like me what to wear. You should take your own advice."

I huffed at him and returned to my cubicle. What woman would want anything to do with him? Who is he talking to? I don't even want to know. I don't know why I bother talking to that jerk.

**Charlene:** *"Girl, Marcus wishes he had a woman with curves like yours. Is the person he is talking to... you?"*

*Wednesday, February 28, 2018*

Marcus's comments about me about dressing nicer have been percolating in my head. It isn't a new thought. I was considering updating my wardrobe. It was already on my spreadsheet. If I choose more flattering outfits for Charlene, we could be in a better place. She could have a spectacular coming out story... like the makeovers in those ugly duckling movies. In reality, all they do is take the glasses off the nerdy girl, put her in a new outfit and let her hair down. The "beauty" was already there. All they change is the window dressing.

I'm clearly not putting my best look forward, if I am looking panda bear-ish. Or like I need to go to the gym as a workout buddy for my fit friend. This couldn't be an elaborate intervention to get me to the gym covertly, right?

If I am being fair, my favorite outfits have been super clingy on me lately. I've been having to suck Charlene in and pull down my top every time I stand up. Plus, my butt has been showing up in my work pants. I know I caught Greg checking me out by the coffee machine. I don't need to be giving the guys at work any ideas with my cleavage wanting to pop out my shirts and my skirts riding up if they get too tight. Now that The Dude and Marcus have me on edge about the guys checking me out, I have been feeling a little paranoid. It does seem like they pop by my cubicle somewhat often and seem to stare at my chest more than I would like. I don't know how I never noticed that before.

Yup, I do need to do some clothes shopping. Most of my working clothes look like I just came out of college. They are the definition of first interview suit, boring blue blazer and pinstripe pants with a light-colored shirt. I think I have three sets of khaki pants, two pencil skirts and four different light-blue tailored shirts. They have also gotten much more close-fitting than I would prefer to wear. I totally could stand to vary my routine and loosen up my shirts, especially if my cleavage is distracting my coworkers.

I have had at least two discussions with HR already about office-appropriate wear, because my office polos were too tight in the bust area. I couldn't button them up, and apparently that caused a stir. Someone complained that I was dressing too sexy for the office. I had requested a larger size than I received. Yet when I had refused to wear the polos previously, I was informed it was required wear. Then at an event, where I was casually asked to be more "appropriate", I ended up having to tie a scarf around my neck to keep HR happy.

This whole business casual dress code is pretty sketchy, anyways. I'm never sure if I'm pushing it too much when I wear jeans to work on Fridays. I never wear any type of fitted jeans. My work jeans are loose-fit black mom jeans to de-emphasize my butt. The guys get away with distressed blue jeans and tight V-neck t-shirts, and no one is calling HR about their clothes, their pecs or their glutes on display. Well, there aren't any of those on display because it is dad bods and beer bellies. But if any of the guys had pecs or glutes worth eyeballing, would anyone be complaining to HR?

Okay, I have convinced myself. I definitely need to buy new clothes, but I think maybe I need some help. I should get a stylist to help me look chic and dress my body. Well, to dress Charlene. I never did find a dress I liked to go to the wedding. I ended up wearing a black sack that didn't do much for me. It didn't even highlight my cleavage, which is arguably my best feature.

**Charlene**: *"Who says your breasts are best? I'm the star feature here. You need a complaints department to complain about HR."*

*Friday, March 2, 2018*

I wonder where my style gene has gone. If women are the gurus of fashion, I missed my allotment.

I decided to quiz Lucy about style, as she always has on the most interesting and colorful ensembles. Today, she was wearing royal purple slacks with a multicolored woven poncho, cinched with a gold belt. Her sandals were gold slingbacks. It was loud, exotic and absolutely a Lucy-look. She's never boring, and while I would never be so daring, I'm impressed by her willingness to dress completely out of the box.

I tried asking her today about her fashion inspiration.

"My friend Michael got me this polo. He has such an eye for finding good stuff in the flea markets. I swear, he has a gift."

Lucy has claimed she naturally has style, because her "people" (her parents) are "from the islands". Her mother is from Trinidad and her father is from Barbados. Although she herself has never traveled to the Caribbean, she attributes all her personality to island vibes.

She launched into an enthusiastic review about the latest designs from the runways in Milan. In the last issue of *Vogue*, she noted that the upcoming trend was to pair ethnic pieces with closet staples. The idea is to bring cultural significance to elevate your look. I expressed confusion over what was an "ethnic" piece.

"Oh, you know, the kinds of things you would get in the tourist shops: woven headbands, leather cuffs, wooden earrings, souvenir stuff like that." My tourist knick-knacks are keychains. I have an impressive collection. I am pretty sure stringing a bunch together and wearing those as bracelets would not elevate my look. I would just be clacking through the office.

Her other recommendation was bold pieces of statement jewelry and earrings. She pointed to her ears, where she was wearing the equivalent of drapery tassels, also multicolored to align with her poncho's ambiguous palette. If I ventured down into the IT section with any part of her ensemble on, it would be to much hooting and hollering from my colleagues. I would be a walking red flag to the noxious, opinionated bulls in my section. Beige and neutrals may be the safest choice, and sadly, elevating my look to Lucy's levels could be detrimental to my workplace health.

"Does no one comment on your outfits to the office?" I wondered if she was ever pulled into an HR meeting to discuss how her cleavage was distracting and a potential risk. She has been featured in the office newsletter for her innovation and creativity and for being the avantgarde face of the company in reception. All of this was code, I guess, for encouraging her for being visibly different and supporting marketing's spin about the forward-thinking roles for women in engineering firms. I'm not as convinced, given that thirty percent of the employees are female, and eighty percent of them are in HR, marketing and administration. There are literally three of us in somewhat technical roles: me in the coding department; one field agent, who is a sales representative; and one support technician, who manages the customer complaints line. My other technical counterparts also exist in a world of beige and neutral polos and slacks. Meanwhile, the rest of the office ladies are colorful fashionistas among the pastels, blues and greens of the men.

Could it be my technical skills have overwritten my fashion genes? Or has following the guys' dress code been a subtle way to protect myself from overt scrutiny and harassment? I'm already required to do more and be more accountable, so dressing more flamboyantly would only give fuel to the criticism.

I'm not sure Lucy's advice will help Charlene and me feel more comfortable at the workplace. Maybe in after-hours looks I could punch up my wardrobe with more colors, ethnic creativity and repurposed household décor.

**Charlene**: *"Girl, you can dress me up how you like. I'm still going to shine on."*

Saturday, March 3, 2018

I was channeling Lucy's fashion sense and decided to just do something different with my hair. So, I tried to order a sexy wig online. I imagined a shoulder-length, sultry brunette curly wig would change my appearance and give some visual interest without being too over-the-top.

The internet is a dangerous place, though. One search into long wigs and suddenly my feed was full of anime cosplay. Neon pinks, pastel blues, gravity-defying ponytails. It was a candy store for hair. I don't think HR polices hair colors, but these might not match our business casual dress codes. Along with the hair, there were suggestions for anime character costumes. I wonder if Dude would go for that.

Charlene was in my head, encouraging me to exude confidence and just go for it. *"Girl, embrace your diva side and let's get wild. Pink is my favorite color... let's do pink hair!"*

Please don't judge. I caved and bought a long pink and white one, and a French maid costume. Not subtle, not work-appropriate. Absolutely not "sexy librarian". It is more like "magical girl who moonlights as a stripper". Why did I buy that one?

I just jumped out of myself for a bit and imagined that I could be as bold as my spunky appendage. I need to have an alter ego that's fun and over-the-top. I'm already imagining The Dude's face when I swish into the room with this cotton candy mane. I wonder if he would laugh and get into it with me. I could do a sexy striptease or something for him.

It is just long enough that it brushes my waist. If I were to dress sexy in some lingerie, would Charlene steal the show? Am I thinking of being sexy for him, or wondering if I can be sexy even with Charlene hogging the spotlight? After all, the belly is the focus in the belly dance act, isn't it? Now I need a coin belt to jiggle along, too, and need watch some tutorial videos on how to belly dance.

**Charlene:** *"Girl, if you're going to do a striptease, don't forget who's center stage. Me. Charlene. I'm the headliner; you're just the supporting act."*

*Tuesday, March 6, 2018*

I think there are different rules for different body shapes and sizes.

Lucy showed up in a super-short skirt today and a diaphanous top that looked like it was stitched together with fairy dust. Her adjustment for modesty was lime-green tights under the whole getup. She gets away with most of her outfits, since she is not overly endowed. If I wore that, it would be mayhem in the coding section. The guys would be standing around my cubicle, razzing me about candy, and undoubtedly, I would get a note from HR reminding me about the dress code.

I'm not even mad that Lucy can wear clothes that would warrant a stern discussion with HR if I tried them. It is that the hypocrisy is so obvious even when there is supposed to be a dress code that applies to everyone. Our office is supposed to be business casual, but that only applies to the men. The women are always held to a higher standard, and especially the well-endowed women. What even is business casual for women? Polos and slacks do not cover the wide variety of choices that women have to make. Are sleeveless dresses okay? Are blazers required?

Meanwhile, the guys can wear pretty much anything they want. Hoodies, sneakers, jeans that look like they survived a world war. No one bats an eye. One Friday, I wore blue jeans and unfortunately for me, senior management just happened to do a walkthrough that morning. Guess who got called into a side office and berated for "not looking professional"?

Know what else? At least two of the other guys were wearing jeans that same day. Apparently, their denim was invisible to the professionalism police. My jeans, however, were a crime against corporate decorum.

This isn't about clothes. It's about policing what women wear. Was I too casual, or not "sexy enough" to make jeans acceptable? The real dress code is: don't make anyone uncomfortable by showing off a body they can't control.

**Charlene:** *"Girl, they don't know what to do with us. If we cover up, we're sloppy. If we show up, we're scandalous. Either way, we're trouble."*

# Five

## IMAGE IS EVERYTHING

Saturday, March 10, 2018

I decided to call an image consultant, Ms. Vivian Fields. I thought image consultants were supposed to help you dress the body you have and make you look just killer in what fits you best and all that. Well, she did help me look killer... like a dream killer.

I read that you need to dress for the job you want, not the one you have. Maybe I should dress like a fashion model, because the outfit of computer programmer is not anyone's dream look, even if it is my dream job. Then again, I watch fashion models and lust after their looks, not the look they are wearing, the way their body is looking. It's not the outfit I want. It's the body *in* the outfit.

I digress, though. This image consultant did not have the same idea as me or Charlene. She met me at my apartment and immediately started checking me out. Awkward. Another woman openly scanning your body with the full intention to dish on you and criticize you is truly disconcerting. I suppose I did give her my tacit permission to tell me everything that's wrong with how I look. Still, it felt odd to be assessed so blatantly and so discouragingly. She asked me to strip to my underwear. Only my mother, The Dude and sometimes my bestie get to see that, and only rarely. The strange woman wanted to get right into it, without even buying me a drink first.

Her first comment, the very first words she said after greeting me: "Well, you know we need to work on that belly. Maybe if you lose a few pounds, your clothes will drape better."

Oh, you mean you think I don't know I'm fat with a belly pouch? Not a great start.

What makes it all worse is that Ms. Vivian Fields is a slim, short, beautiful black woman. Even though her edges are laid and her weave goes down to her waist, she did not dress like I imagined a black person would. She was wearing a peach twinset over pale green capri pants, very Alicia Silverstone in *Clueless* or the classic Stepford wife. It worked on her and she did look polished, but her style did not mesh with mine. If I dressed like her, I would look like a pastel lollipop.

Still, I shrugged off the growing despair that this was not going to work. She was a professional. Surely her recommendations would match my needs. We stood in front of my mirror and she started preaching about knowing my colors. Are we still in the 80s, draping shawls over each other looking for brightness? Apparently, yes.

She said that earth tones are too muddy on me and I should wear bright colors. Hmmm, why would I want to call attention to my non-model body? Black is slimming, everyone knows that.

I was resistant, but nodded along when she told me that pastels wash me out, and primary colors enliven my skin.

Orange, peach and yellow should be my best friends, and pink, but only hot pink, would balance my red undertone. Avoid red tones and rosy pinks as it makes me look blotchy. She said all this with authority, but it all looked the same to me.

Charlene was excited: she wanted the full makeover experience. *"Let's get more color in the wardrobe. I want to get my vogue on! Yes to hot pink. All eyes will be on me!"*

Meanwhile, Ms. Fields scanned my wardrobe with barely hidden distaste, not saying much but lifting her eyebrows and shaking her head.

"You don't opt for very feminine choices," she murmured. "Do you not like to wear dresses?"

There is an actual halter dress hanging in the back of my closet that I love, but it doesn't love me back. I also think it is a size (or two) too small now. Also, that's not appropriate for work. I had specified that I wanted a new *work* wardrobe.

I work with a bunch of guys. I don't need to be looking like a sweet little lady. I need to look like "I'm here to work on code, just like the rest of the crew".

She asked me to pick out my favorite outfits and try them on for her. I showed her some geometric patterned tunics in blue and green, and, of course, my slimming pinstriped pants. My true favorite is a much-loved dark wash bootcut jeans, paired with an abstract brown and white mesh fabric top that I used to wear with a black camisole for casual Fridays. The jeans are super tight now and make my butt look great, so it's no longer in the work rotation. It also shows off my muffin top and the camisole isn't long enough to cover Charlene very well. I still like the mesh top, though, but I hardly wear that pair of jeans anymore, anywhere.

In all honesty, my faves (work and otherwise) don't fit like I want them to anymore, but I hold on to them in hope... in earnest prayer for a miracle. But Ms. Fields wasn't in love with anything I showed her.

"Even if these fit again when you work on your tummy," she said, "they don't suit you." OUCH!

"You need some pantsuits and some jackets with bright colors for the shells. Yes, maybe even a colorful pant, like hot pink pant with a yellow shell. Think of yourself like a flower in bloom. Tie it together with a tan blazer to keep it professional," she dictated.

I was thinking, *I'm going to be a walking target of mockery.*

Charlene was drinking this up. *"I'm not a simple flower in bloom. I'm a succulent, carrying all the resources to keep shining, and my flower is rare and beautiful."*

What the hell? That spiel was not landing well with me. Are image consultants offering hypnosis sessions for personality overhauls, too? Why not actually try to match my personality and lifestyle in the here and now, not if I want to audition for a body swap movie? I can't believe I paid for this level of criticism. I'm almost depressed enough to commit to going to the gym with Tanya to start working on my belly.

I had a built-in cheerleader urging me to keep up with this makeover attempt.

**Charlene**: *"Chin up, girl. Don't get discouraged. Trust the process. I'm going to look fabulous."*

*Wednesday, March 14, 2018*

My next appointment with the image consultant was thankfully an online meeting. We needed to discuss our tactics and the overall look for me. She told me how truly excited she was to go shopping with me. I believed her. I guessed she loved shopping, or more specifically, loved shopping with other people's money. We agreed on spending about $1,000 for a capsule wardrobe. I am wondering if the diet capsules as seen on TV would be a better investment than these painful sessions of, "You just don't look good in clothes." Still, she went on... schedule a makeup session and maybe a haircut. I balked again. I just wanted to know what clothes will make me look twenty pounds slimmer, not get set up in a *People* magazine-style makeover.

I grudgingly agreed to meet her at the mall next Saturday, but my spirits were low. Instead of feeling buoyed by having a cheerleader in my corner, I felt like the hot girl in school is looking at me like a sad project. I already suspected I wasn't going to like how it all turns out in the end. The first in-person consultation cost me $500 and cued up an evening of emotional eating of bread sticks and ice cream, while pondering my life choices.

I now had a running spreadsheet of ways to improve my life and so far, all my attempts were crashing. This online session had no additional charge, but it was a continuation of the slow, self-esteem-strangling torture. I was left with the growing feeling of discontent that made me wish I could cancel this whole process, just like that damn gym membership, which is also still haunting me.

The Dude gave me mixed messages when I shared my personal shopper plan, and the whole miserable experience of it so far. He thought it was great that I was updating my wardrobe but he also agreed that I need to lose some weight around my belly.

"Don't get mad at me. I know it bothers you about your weight and your stomach, so it's not my opinion. I want you to be happy with how you look. So, get some new clothes and do whatever makes you feel good about your body," he said. He tried to reassure me. It sounded good when he explained it, but it still feels like he isn't sure what to say to me.

I just want to feel like I'm not being judged for a body part that I cannot seem to control. Charlene is like a sixth finger. Unless I want to get surgery to cut her off, she's just a part of me.

Maybe The Dude is right… because I am conflicted, he is conflicted about what to tell me.

**Charlene**: *"Girl, just listen to me. The Dude agrees that you should show off what you got. I'm not a hidden feature. No guts, no glory!"*

*Saturday, March 17, 2018*

I met the image consultant at the mall. She watched my boyfriend jeans and loose tunic with a frown. It is not even a distressed jean, I thought. I dressed for comfort, and something easy to take on and off. This is not a runway show, I told myself.

"Wearing baggy clothes just makes you look bigger. Didn't we talk about using a belt to highlight your midsection? Anyways, we will deal with that as we shop," she said. I already felt two inches tall.

Honestly, I tried a dress with a belt to incorporate her rules. The cotton maxi dress was loose and flowy, but when belted, I looked like the Michelin's man's wife, all rolls. I want to love my current body, not frown at it. I got discouraged and decided jeans and a tunic were the answer. Now with Ms. Fields's disapproving stare heavy on me, I already felt like this shopping trip was going to be problematic.

"Let's go into Macy's," she said. "We will start with some basic dresses to get you going." I was not surprised at all when she started pulling out the illusion dresses with the black curvy panels on the sides and bright solid panels in the center front and back. On our online call, she had already discussed these sheath dresses as being a basic work necessity in my female body armor.

Instead of my real size 16, she told me to try on size 14. She claimed my clothes need to skim my body, not hide it. My clothes should also not cling to me in loud, squealing desperation, I thought. Doesn't she understand my need not to feel squeezed into my clothes? I'd also like to eat a donut and not think the seams will pop. She thought I was exaggerating my dress size and wearing too-big clothes. Nope. There was no "give" in the stretchy fabric dress she handed to me.

When I inched the dressing room door open to show her the sad reality, she suggested, "Wearing some shapewear would have been a good idea while trying on these clothes. It improves the fit."

I have heard the fairy tale about good foundation garments before. My mother believed in the power of half-slips and good underwear. The magic stockings of the modern world unfortunately do not have the fat-erasing power of the good ole days. The new mover on the girdle market is Spanx and I have tried to like it. It does not like me.

Charlene and I are both agreed on Spanx. Flesh tubing is not the answer to any of life's mysteries, and it is not a magic marker to erase fat. I don't need help choosing clothes that would look good if I lost five more pounds. I already have that in the back of my closet. This was exactly what I wanted to avoid.

We went on to look at the hot pink pants that she so dearly loves for me. It looked like it was made for Barbie, and it was a straight cut, too. No accommodation for any rear appendages. Thankfully, there weren't any in my size at all. She ruefully picked out an olive-green version and said, "Try this to see how it fits. We can always order the color we want online."

I was good with the green, which seemed more normal. This time, the size 16 didn't fit either my jelly belly or my ass. A nice salesgirl came to my rescue and brought me a size 20 and said, "Trust me. That cut runs small." Now, the salesgirl, I absolutely trusted her. She was a curvy thing and she looked skeptically at the cute pixie trying to pick out my clothes, in completely the wrong sizes. It was obvious to us that Ms. Fields had never had to shop in the plus-size section for herself or anyone else. We did not have the same figure challenges.

Us big girls recognize each other. The size 20 fit, and what was better, it made my butt look great. One foundation piece in the bag. Woohoo!

Ms. Fields looked at me and my olive-green pant with much less enthusiasm. "Well, we'll just punch this up with a bright pink top."

I wanted to punch her out. She brought me a pink chiffon blousy bit with lovely long sleeves and rouching. I was thinking that the sleeves would cover my bat wings. Alas, when I put it on, it was a crop top.

"Where's the rest of this top? I can't be showing my belly fat," I protested.

"This look is so in now," she said as she grimaced at me. "You could try it with a high-waisted capri, which will cover your, uh, problem areas...."

I watched her, totally baffled. How was she helping me by suggesting clothes that would never look good on the body that I have right now?

"No. I don't want any high-waisted pants." I insisted, "Let's find another top that covers my belly. This top is just too short."

She interrupted. "No, you need to find tops that stop right at your waist. Longer tops will just make you look like a rectangle with no shape."

Hey, rectangle is a shape and if that's the shape I have, what else are we supposed to do? That's what I was thinking. I mumbled something to get her to stop staring balefully at me.

I was getting tired of this whole shit.

I could practically hear Charlene mouthing off to me, *"I am all about a style makeover, but this woman is buying clothes to suit* her *body and tastes, not accent* ours. *She's misreading the inputs. You should terminate her contract now."*

"I think we have enough pieces for my capsule. Let's call it a day," I told Ms. Fields as I moved toward the registers.

We got two "illusion dresses", where the only illusion is that anyone believed I look slimmer in them. The green pants, and an orange and pink floral maxi skirt that looks so huge I could wear it as a tent dress. She suggested wearing an orange camisole with it and actually picked out a tangerine orange tank with some beading. How is a cotton camisole $50, I think. Are those beads made of real gold?

If I do wear the maxi skirt, I would pair it with a nice blousy shirt and then I would cinch it with a belt. Actually, nope. I would not wear the belt and just keep it all loose and flowy. You can't unbelt your clothes over lunch. That's not a good look.

There was a tan jacket that she was miffed at because it stops at my hip. It came with matching pants, which I was happy to purchase. She scoffed at the lack of color in all my choices.

"Make sure you wear a bright color with it."

I was absolutely thinking of a brown camisole.

There were two other chiffon tops with long bell sleeves, one yellow with red and orange embroidery in a panel over my chest and the other, peach with some kind of romantic (her word) red lacings on the sides. Both thankfully go down to my actual waist. I was still hesitant that I would ever wear them.

She threw in some chunky necklaces to add interest and draw eyes up to my pretty face. Yeah. "You're fat, but you have such a pretty face." I've heard that line so many times I always write off the speaker from the moment they spew it at me.

I personally picked out two colorfully patterned leggings. One looks like a galaxy print and the other met her guidelines. It has flowers on it, giant red roses. She asked what those were for when I put them on the checkout counter. I told her they would be workout gear.

She beamed at my answer. "Great. You're following the style rules even with your gym clothes. You get it."

Honestly, I totally plan to wear these leggings with one of my long black tunics to go everywhere when I feel too fat for jeans. Gym wear is baggy t-shirts and plain leggings. Why would I pay $30 a pair to sweat in these beauties?

Anyways, that was my haul for $1,000, plus the $200 I had to pay her for her time as a shopping assistant to make me feel fat and frumpy.

"So, when will we do the makeup and hair session?" she asked.

"Let my bank account catch up and I will call you." We both laughed at that. I was laughing because I already knew I hope to never talk to this woman again. She was probably just laughing at me. What a schmuck I am.

**Charlene:** *"Girl, it's not the clothes. She just wasn't the right fit for you. Chin up and belly up."*

*Friday, March 23, 2018*

Did it bring me joy?

I didn't even try on those clothes from our shopping trip for over a week. That tells you how good I felt about myself after that little escapade. I hated that I spent almost $2,000 to feel fatter and less attractive than ever. I hated that I bought clothes that didn't bring me JOY, per Marie Kondo. It was all such a huge hit to my self-esteem that I wondered if Charlene gained five pounds in revenge for thinking I could hide her.

When I did pull out the clothes, they looked even worse at home than in the store. As it happened, everything hung the wrong way on my body, clutching at all my fatty bits, and I just felt more frustrated. My mean mirror had me contort in all directions, yet there was no flattering angle. Is there some illusion lighting in store dressing rooms or do they have the fun house mirrors that make you look longer and slimmer?

If they do sell those kinds of mirrors, I want one!!! I need one for my home closet, my bathroom, and pretty much everywhere mirrors exist. They should switch all mirrors everywhere to ones that make it look like we all lost a few inches. Millions of dollars in therapy could be saved if we just matched on the outside what we think we look like on the inside.

When I found those lovely leggings at the bottom of the bag I sighed happily. At least I have two new friends... fancy fashionable leggings, and not transparent like the expensive sheer leggings that went viral. So, take that!!!

Do you know what did bring me joy? Sending an email to Ms. Fields letting her know that I no longer needed her services. I should have also told her that she could not seem to separate her idea of what looked good on her with what the client, ME, needed to look good. She was eager to spend someone else's money to indulge her shopping habits. Sadly, I didn't write that. I wrote that I think we made a good start on my wardrobe revamp.

Charlene was in my head, encouraging me to stand up more for myself. I took the first step. I decided I can choose my own clothes without seeing Ms. Fields' sneer or hearing her comments on my belly. I'm in control of my image and the Stepford wife look is not it. Classy, casual and comfortable is my plan.

**Charlene**: *"Girl, I would look amazing in hot pink. But for now, you don't need anything other than stretchy leggings and a caramel milkshake."*

*Saturday, March 24, 2018*

Okay, I pulled up my big, big-girl panties and decided to go shopping again. This time, I went alone, without the voice of criticism in my ear. Well, without Ms. Fields' criticisms, as I had enough of my own. I tried, really tried to not just buy boring beige and overly big clothes. I selected some of the outfits I saw styled on the plus-sized mannequins. There was a peachy floral shirt with a self-tie belted waist, paired with striped green and brown pants with a long rise, which looked classy and put together. The look didn't feel like me, but it was the spring palette Ms. Fields suggested. I was trying to push myself out of the comfort zone and into the style zone.

I had to take a couple size options with me into the fitting room because I have trust issues about size tags now. The point is not the size anyway. It is about the fit. Finally, I had a look that screamed "someone else dressed me today". I was hoping that was a noticeable improvement over my usual look. To test the theory, I arranged a date with The Dude to meet up at his favorite Chinese buffet.

I wanted him to see me "out in the wild", as I was feeling pretty out of my element. I wondered why everyone wasn't giving me a double take because I looked different. Did anyone notice I was dressed in brighter colors and wearing a higher-waisted pant? Wasn't this improved color palette supposed to make me glow and stop traffic? I was promised at least a double take by some passably attractive guy, even if I didn't cause any road traffic accidents.

The greeter at the restaurant didn't look at me any differently. We are almost regulars to that place. We eat there far too often and I didn't even get a head nod of acknowledgment from our usual server. So maybe I was expecting a lot from The Dude. I was hoping he'd make a comment, a compliment, but he didn't say anything.

"Hey, I'm over here. Why didn't you let me pick you up? It seems like a waste of gas for us to drive separately," The Dude said.

"I thought we could try something new. It's good to change things up, don't you think? Like, try a different dish today. What looks good, anything caught your eye?" I said.

I tried to be coy. Basically, I threw some hints at him to see if he would pick up on me looking, feeling different. He almost got it. Slurping on some shrimp, he asked me, "Did something happen in work today? Did Tanya call again, or Marcus? You're acting strange."

"No, I'm not. I just wondered if you noticed anything different today?"

"Oh, are you talking about cutting your hair again? You did say you wanted to change it. I don't mind. It's your hair. You can do anything you like." The Dude continued eating his surf and turf plate without pause. I sighed.

"No. I didn't change my hair. What do you think about my clothes?" I asked.

"What about them?" he asked.

"What do you think of my look? I changed up my style." I told him.

"Babes, you always look good to me. You know you don't have to dress up to impress me. Also, could you pass the steak sauce?"

Color theory be damned. The Dude did not notice any change in my style. Sigh.

**Charlene**: *"Girl, the only thing he would notice is the extra serving of hot fudge on the soft serve ice cream. With me as the cherry on top of his hot girlfriend sundae."*

*Monday, March 26, 2018*

Do I look pregnant?

Marketing came through the office today hoping to take some photos to include in the employee newsletter. They do this a couple times of the year, looking for the token minorities to feature. I always get called out because I am the lone female engineer working with all those guys. I wasn't even fazed because I was wearing one of my new outfits. Today, it was a lime-green pinstriped blouse with "feminizing ruffles" on the shoulder sleeve seam, paired with a tan pencil skirt. Nothing too remarkable for the guys to comment on, but relatively fashion forward. This time, I felt that marketing and I could put a good face out there.

Ms. Marketing, as always, looked extra encouragingly toward me. "Oh good, we can feature you along with our accommodations for our working mothers."

I was confused. First, do we even have accommodations for anyone besides the C-suite? Also, none of us in the technical department are parents at all. Who can have children and work these crazy hours? She clarified her comments and torpedoed my confidence with her next words. "When are you due?" she asked. What??? She thought my burrito belly was a baby in the making! Omigod... I felt so dumb and so fat.

Charlene wanted me to stand up and reply, "*I'm not pregnant, but we're due for a promotion and an espresso machine in the breakroom. That would be great accommodations for your star coding team!*"

Marcus watched my face and smirked. I was mortified and excused myself to the restroom. I looked at myself in the mirror and wondered what did everyone else see. I turned to the side and doubted that this could be a belly bump.

The marketing team got what they needed without me, because I took an extended coffee break and didn't return for their shoot. I was not going to be insulted and photographed looking like I was ready to proceed to the maternity ward. When Marcus messaged that the coast was clear, it was close to quitting time. I came up for my bag, and to take my rotund belly out of the building. Marcus was still laughing at me. He was about to fall off his chair.

"If you had seen your face when she asked you that. I wish I could have that as my screensaver."

Marcus is such an ass. I cannot even deal with him right now.

**Charlene**: *"Girl, pregnant bellies are celebrated for making women glow. So, glow up and show up proudly. Stop hiding. Don't get mad, get preening!"*

## *Six*

# I THOUGHT HE WAS SUPPORTIVE

Wednesday, March 28, 2018

Is he for me or against me?

My boyfriend has pet names for Charlene too... he's always called her his little pillow. Sometimes he calls her his marshmallow. It makes me feel warm and wonderful, thinking that he has accepted her. If he can claim her and name her... why not me?

I had been feeling a little low about the image consultant debacle The Dude chastised me over the amount of money I spent on Ms. Fields, saying I could have paid him to choose my clothes. I didn't bother to share the pregnancy thing, because I didn't need to hear any reinforcements of those comments. Instead, I started giving some more thought to the gym suggestion. Maybe instead of dressing Charlene, I do indeed need to work her off of me. Still, I thought The Dude liked me, liked my body just as it was, even if he always agrees that if I could spot reduce it would be great.

"Tanya still wants me to go to the gym with her. I can't imagine a worse use of my Friday nights, sweating on the Stairmaster or some other evil piece of gym equipment," I said. I knew I was whining but I thought he would say something supportive, like I don't need to go to the gym. He is as uplifting as a wireless bra, which means, not really. The good thing is that he doesn't poke me in the ribs, most of the time. He is comfortable and warm and good at hugging me. Apparently, he is also good at convincing me I would look good next to him in a gym because The Dude got all excited and said, "Yeah. Didn't we agree to upgrade your membership to a group plan? You don't need to go with Tanya. We can work out together, babes. I got all the tips from Mike on working with weights to make some gains. You know, the couple that gyms together, gains together."

*Who are you and where did my lazy dude go?* I thought. I forgot that he had a man crush on his Muscle Milk buddy Mike. Apparently, he also decided he needed to be a muscle man. How is it I'm suddenly surrounded by all these fitness freaks? He used to be the one to have a fit when I said let's take a walk and stop drinking soda.

As it happened, when we stopped sodas, he also dropped twenty pounds and I was, like, what did you do? As you guessed, nothing happened to my weight. Admittedly, I didn't drink that much soda before. I liked fruit juices and I switched to drinking more water. I started to pee all the time with all the water I was drinking. I have trained my bladder now to hold 16 ounces, because I really go when I go, if you know what I mean. People are, like, stunned in the bathroom cubicles when they realize that I'm seriously peeing so long. It is kind of embarrassing.

Sometimes I won't even use the office bathroom if there are too many people in there. I'll just pretend to touch up my face, leave and then come back after about ten minutes.

It was my mistake for bringing up the gym again, even to complain. My dude wants us to go to the gym as a couple. I'm going to be dragged into this gym membership by love or friendship. Maybe this is what the universe is trying to tell me. Okay, Charlene, it seems like we are meant to have abs or die trying.

**Charlene**: *"The Dude is angling to spend more time together. He loves me, girl. You need to join the Charlene fan club."*

Gym day one and what would you know, The Dude, who I shall now call Mr. Strong, has hurt his shoulder or pulled a ligament. He was such a show-off. We went to the gym and I said,

"Let's warm up on the treadmill."

I started off with a brisk stroll, but he cranked his speed way up and was pelting down the treadmill like he's running the 100m with Usain Bolt. I asked, "Who is chasing after you?"

"Why are you being a granny, going so slow. Get your heart rate up." Mr. Strong huffed at me.

Needless to say, he didn't even make five minutes on the treadmill before he was done. I, meanwhile, was happily jogging along on my 30-minute program of hills. Next, I heard him clanging away on one of those weight machines. I finished my warmup and he was nursing his shoulder. He was trying to lift 200 pounds on some rowing equipment, determined to lift his body weight. Really, on day one?

"Why didn't you start light and work your way up to it?" I asked.

"That's not how it's done, babes. You have to max out the weight. Remember, I've been reading those fitness magazines. You don't know anything about how to get fit. That's why I'm here to guide you," The Dude said, grimacing as he rolled his shoulders.

"Well, I knew enough not to hurt myself at the gym," I said. All I did was warm up for thirty minutes, and he was ready to leave.

Since he was hurt, and I am a supportive girlfriend, we left. Well, things do work out for the best. I didn't even want to be there, but now I can totally tell Tanya I went to the gym, too. It wasn't as bad as I remembered from the past. I remember always feeling pretty self-conscious on those trips. Gym enthusiasts are a whole different breed. When I go, I feel like a fish out of water, and not the cool, flexible, "everybody loves dolphins" kind of fish. I am more of the gasping for air, floundering on dry land, scaly and mostly scary-looking kind of fish. This time, though, I was so distracted by my dude's antics that I stopped worrying about my own insecurities. If anyone was even looking at me, I didn't notice. If only just for a distraction, a gym buddy might be a good idea after all.

In our brief time at the gym, I realized that men are awfully proud of their man boobs. They were walking around bare chested as if their "moobs" were pecs. They posed in front of the mirrors to flex and it seemed as if the mirror action pumped up their self-esteem as well. Meanwhile, I was trying my best not to look at my sweaty reflection because I was not at all enthused to see my non-muscle-fatty bits.

Even my dude got into the action. He was checking out his barrel chest in the mirror and grunting loudly with every curl/lift/bench press. Could it be a competitive form of preening, all this alpha male grunting?

Come to think about it, the whole gym outing was some kind of competition for him. He had to look strong so he had to push his body weight and run full out instead of slowly warming up. Maybe *Men's Fitness* needs to do an article on competing with yourself instead of the other gym blokes. I know if I said as much to him, he wouldn't take me seriously.

Still, I wonder what I need to do to make my bathroom mirror pump me up as effectively as the gym mirrors do for the guys. I could do with some positive reinforcement from my reflection.

The gym mirror didn't do much for me. I felt it was being very passive aggressive, reinforcing my absolute fatness, showing me my rolls from every angle, everywhere I looked. Very judgy mirrors, reflecting me and Charlene in the worst possible light. I would know smug and judgy because I am pretty judgmental myself. I don't need to look at myself or Charlene in that many mirrors for so long.

Again, where do they sell the circus mirrors that slim you down? I want to install some in the damn gym.

**Charlene**: *"I was checking myself out in the mirror and I think I look great. Perfection is a matter of perception."*

*Wednesday, April 4, 2018*

It was my birthday today and it totally sucked. No bikinis or martinis can be blamed.

I had to work. There was another server crash after an overnight software update. We spent the whole day restoring the system to pre-update status and block the automatic update from re-installing. This means I worked through lunch while fielding calls from everyone who was pissed that we kept the server offline until we isolated the programs. How do they expect me to work on the problem if they keep calling every fifteen minutes to work on said problem?

The guys were being pissy as always, because they get even more bitchy when things go wrong. When we finally got the server problem all sorted, about two hours before close of work, I get a new employee setup request for the next morning. Those usually fall to me so that the guys don't scare off the new employees with their lack of people skills.

Unfortunately, that also meant I had to work late, on top of everything else. Greg offered to stay and help me by rubbing my shoulders. I had tried reporting him to HR about two weeks ago. They assured me they would speak to the team, but also reminded me that I needed to account for the fact that it was an all-male environment. Basically, I was told I shouldn't be so touchy about jokes. I scowled at Greg and stared at him like he had grown another head. He got the hint and left me to it. I didn't leave the office until almost seven p.m.

I had planned to meet up with Marcus and The Dude for some after-work drinks, but that couldn't happen. I sent The Dude a text saying that I was working late. All he replied was a thumbs up. No message of commiseration. No offer to bring me cheer-up donuts or any other kind of sustenance. No protest about a possible birthday dinner being canceled. I thought he forgot.

It turned out he had sent some flowers, lovely yellow Easter lilies. Those are my favorite flowers. The sad thing is that the flowers had arrived in the morning at the apartment complex office. They were wrapped in cellophane and not in a vase. The office staff didn't put them in water or anything for me. When I got home, frustrated, hangry and feeling sorry for myself, my lily bouquet was looking wilted and brown. It looked how I felt.

The real kicker was the stupid card that The Dude attached. We usually give each other funny cards, but this one missed the mark. There was a picture of a whale on the front and the message read: "Just like Greenpeace, I love whales. Happy birthday."

He loves whales? What is he trying to tell me with such a stupid card?

Now I have to commit to going to the gym so I can work off Charlene and all this whale blubber. So much for loving my body.

I would have preferred if he had just forgotten my birthday instead of finding a whale card.

Charlene and I celebrated myself with a tub of Häagen-Dazs Dulce de Leche. No whales and no dudes were harmed for my birthday.

**Charlene**: *"Girl, we can celebrate all month if you like. You have my back and I have your front. We're solid."*

*Thursday, April 5, 2018*

**<Did you like it?>**

I woke up to a message from The Dude and I was completely confused. Was he asking if I liked his stupid card and flowers?

**<No, that was a stupid card and you know that.>** I messaged back, while blowing on my coffee mug. I included angry emojis to let him know I was serious. I didn't appreciate the whale reference, not even as a bad joke.

**<What do you mean? You love Greenpeace.>**
**<You called me a whale! That was not funny.>**

My mood was still sour from my not-great birthday, and ice cream also hadn't been a great choice for dinner. I needed coffee, bacon, bread and cheese and some me time. I had already decided I was going into the office late. I was going to take my compensatory time, because once I stepped foot in that office it would be Armageddon all over again. The boys could handle all the post-server reset complaints. I was not in the mood. I needed some couch time watching *House Hunters International*, and imagining my future tropical escape.

The Dude called as I was pulling the bacon from the fridge.

"Why are you being like that about a silly card? I was asking about the present, though. Did I do a good job on your bookshelf?" The Dude sounded exasperated, and I couldn't understand why he was the one upset. I had the shit birthday and the shittier card. What was his problem? Also, what bookshelf was he talking about?

"I don't have a bookshelf. I must also have not had enough coffee this morning, because I don't know what you are talking about."

"What time did you get in last night? Didn't you notice the shelf? I had time to assemble it and clean up before you got in. You can tell me what you think of it later. I have to go. We're about to start the maintenance turnaround for the backup generators. Hope you have a good day, babes."

It was a typical call from him. He wanted a quick answer. The Dude wasn't much of a talker or a doer, except when he was at work. Then I imagined he barked orders and did stuff, because he was always busy. I still didn't notice any shelf... well, not in the kitchen.

I wandered into my living room and then I finally understood. He had gotten me a bookshelf, a lovely four-shelf leaning-ladder style shelf. On the shelf, he had also randomly stacked the small tower of books which had been growing on the floor next to my spot on the couch. While he watched crime dramas and action movies, I usually read.

This bookshelf, though, was exactly the kind of thing I should have expected from him. He saw that I needed some storage and he got it for me. It was such a practical and thoughtful gift. Now I needed to organize the books so they looked nice on the shelf. I had underestimated and misjudged The Dude.

I started sorting the books and noticed there was even a new book. He had bought me Isaac Asimov's short story collection. It was the perfect gift. We had re-watched the Will Smith movie, *I, Robot* and I insisted the original Asimov story had to be better. My sweet guy found it and got it for me. He knows me so well.

My day was looking up.

**Charlene**: *"Girl, The Dude may be clueless at picking cards, but at least he can put together a shelf."*

*Friday, April 6, 2018*

Well, I can't win at quitting the gym.

When I told Tanya that my dude hurt himself in the gym, she was eager to take his place on our group gym pass. Yes, I paid to upgrade my membership instead of figuring out the secret code on how to cancel. I'm not sure if we got ourselves locked into the contract for a whole other year with the upgrade. Since I'm paying for it anyway, I agreed with Tanya, somebody ought to use it. She reasoned that we could hang out like we used to, and she still wanted to help train me.

I was happy to let her have his pass because The Dude was stretched out on the couch, insisting he needed to let his tendons heal. After one day in the gym... he is such a dramatist. I was looking forward to spending some quality time with my bestie. We hadn't been spending as much time together as we used to. I could definitely blame that on The Dude. He wasn't much for bars and clubs. He was a homebody. Since he loves whales and I'm still mad about that, I was happy to leave him home and go work my blubber off.

Going to the gym with Tanya was different and totally intense. She is like a fitness fairy godmother, except instead of a wand, she waves around kettlebells and resistance bands. It started off well. We were on the same page with a slow warmup on the treadmill. While she wasn't gunning it on her machine, I did feel some pressure to get into a little bit of a faster jog early on. I was sweating after my warmup, but felt accomplished. Then she suggested we do a class. Zumba was on and I was there and down for that. Let's dance away some pounds; that's my kind of workout. Fun, right? So, we did that and I thought, great, we were done. Nope, she wanted to go do an upper body circuit after, because we only did cardio with the Zumba. Now I'm sweaty and my arms hurt. I wonder if I could tell her I pulled a tendon, too.

We were in the gym for two whole hours. That's too much of my life gone on getting sweaty. Tanya is a beast, a fitness beast, but she is not a whale. Neither am I, or at least I'm trying not to be one.

She was cheerful and encouraging and relentless. This could work. Maybe this will work.

**Charlene**: *"If you insist on going to the gym, I'm on board with making it a dance party. Zumba, yay!"*

*Saturday, April 7, 2018*

OMG! I might have overdone the workout yesterday. I thought those Zumba classes would be just an awesome dance party. It was, but I was terrible at it. I was clumsily jumping around and shaking things that ought not to be shook in other people's faces. The worst part is, now everything hurts.

Even Charlene hurts and there isn't even muscle there, but every time I jiggle, her fat hurts. I can't bend. I can't sit. I went to the toilet and sat there thinking of where I could install grab bars. I wished I had some to pull myself back up as it was too painful to try to stand. Even just lifting my hands to comb my hair felt like punishment so I kept it in a messy ponytail. *Vogue* keeps saying lived-in hair is in style, so that's my excuse.

They've said beauty comes with pain, but this is ridiculous. But at least I am up and walking around.

Meanwhile, my darling boyfriend has claimed he caught a flu bug. He was so sick that he had to come to my house for dinner and spend the night so I could take care of him. I had to show him some love, since he did put together my sweet bookshelf for me. But I don't believe he's truly sick at all. If he was, shouldn't he be worried about exposing me to his germs? To be more convincing, he moaned and rolled around my bed this morning and never left to make it to work. Snowflake.

Just to stick it to him, I asked if he was going to the gym today. I wonder if I'm evil enough to myself to go alone to prove a point. Nah, not a chance. This gym scene is not the life I envisioned for myself. I am envisioning myself in a hammock swaying on the beach listening to that upbeat soca music. All the beautiful island people are eating mangoes, drinking coconut water and taking it easy, man. That's the life for me.

**Charlene**: *"Girl, this is not the way. If we were meant to run, we would have four legs instead of just two. Maybe try something less painful next time. We can dance or work out, not both."*

Sunday, April 8, 2018

Okay, I didn't go back to the gym today, either. I figured you are supposed to take a rest day anyway. Tanya called to ask what time we were going in. I explained that even my smile was hurting from our workout yesterday. She went ahead without me.

My boyfriend is still faking he's sick. It seems the flu hurt his back and that has nothing to do with poor lifting technique in the gym. Meanwhile, he's been chugging Muscle Milk like it's Popeye's spinach super strength formula. He assured me that the protein shakes are nothing short of magical for gains. They try to disguise the taste of chalk (and fail), but he seems to love them. He even tried to tell me the Mr. Olympia contestants are on the same regime for two months before competition, like he is anywhere near bodybuilding physique.

I would laugh at him, except Charlene is still hurting from my Zumba class two days ago. Seems like I might have some muscle underneath there after all. Maybe even I have Ms. Olympia abs.

Hahahaha.

I would drink some of his Muscle Milk, but it's not allowed on the color diet anyways. It also tastes like chalky sadness. They dare to label it as a meal replacement drink. Give me a real meal, thank you. I also suspect it is carb-loaded too, but I'll keep that thought to myself. I have had enough lectures from Mr. Strong about *Men's Fitness* recommendations.

**Charlene**: *"All we are missing now is the rum punch to go along with the hammock and the coconut trees."*

*Seven*

# HOT GUYS MAKE GIRLS SWEAT

*Wednesday, April 11, 2018*

Did you know there's a special term for the belly fat area? It's called the panniculus or the belly apron. I like the term 'belly apron'. It gives the idea of Charlene as being a cute little French maid frilly thing in front of my real girly bits. It's actually almost sexy when you think of it that way. I'm covering up my lady bits with some fleshy modesty. *wink wink*

Now panniculus, that sounds like some special breakfast saucepan. Maybe you can make specialty pancakes in the panniculus. Though to be honest, it was probably those blueberry pancakes and bacon-stuffed Belgian waffles that turned Charlene into that sexy panniculus.

Oh, maybe she is a kind of succubus. You know, those extra-sexy women that suck men in and they can't detach. Yup,

I love that bit the best. Between the French maid analogy and succubus, this is what Charlene personifies.

*"Ooooh, oui, cherie... I am so sexy. I identify as a sexy French maid now. Sexy isn't a size, it's an attitude and I've got it."*

Anyway, I learned those terms from the trainer, Chad, who did my introductory assessment. Since my dude "got hurt" and Tanya wasn't free, I surprised myself and I belly-ed up to the gym by myself. While signing in, I was chatting with the front desk guy about my previous lack of gym attendance.

I learned a lot. Most important, I learned that every year I had been a member of the gym made me eligible for two free training sessions. Now I have five more to go. Yes, it has been that long that I have been paying for this shit and not using it. This also means I will definitely go the gym five more times as I now have weekly appointments with Chad, the trainer, and he will be expecting to see me.

Chad is your stereotypical trainer type. He's hunky if you're into over-the-top muscles and chiseled like The Rock. Of course, his t-shirt and gym shorts were grabbing onto his muscles till you could just about trace the veins on his arms. The first session with Chad wasn't bad at all. We spent most of the time talking about my fitness goals. *Oh, to look like Beyoncé and yeah, I don't want to be skinny, I just want to get toned... blah, blah blah.* All the usual lies we tell ourselves and our hunky gym trainers.

The best part of today's session was that he showed me a thirty-minute quick circuit area that gives you a whole-body workout in minimum time. This is totally my kind of workout. Now, why did Chad say this is only meant for the days when I don't want to work out, and for the people who work out over their lunch hour? What? Exercise instead of eat, who does that?

Also, the days I don't want to work out, that's every day. And if I don't want to work out, why am I coming to the gym at all?

Whatever he might call it, I thought it was the perfect setup for me and I didn't hurt as much after as when I did the Zumba class. This is my kind of gym routine. I was celebrating this first session as my small victory. Chad told me to note my non-scale victories as those are the best kind. However, it is on the scale that we will measure success. Again, Chad can say this because his scale doesn't heave, puff and start to smoke when it is stepped on.

When I got back home, I was still feeling inspired, so I went online and bought a red bikini!! I can barely believe it myself. It is not teenie-weenie body-floss kind of bikini. It is a ruffled, flirty two piece designed for curvy ladies. I still don't know if I will ever wear it, but at least I own one. Why did I buy it? Well, blame it on Chad. He said I needed a motivational objective to keep me focused on my workout goals. I should have the picture or the object itself hanging where I could see it daily. This would help me visualize my success path and help me get into the zone. While I was grunting through the leg presses, he kept telling me to visualize the goal and see my future self. I was visualizing Charlene and me in a hammock on a tropical island. In that vision, Chad was bringing me tropical cocktails, not handing me dumbbells. We were clearly not seeing the same vision.

Since a bikini debacle started this, I figured that would be the perfect goal object, to get me into that tropical vision. I'm now committed to having a bikini-ready body sometime in the future. This torture I'm inflicting on myself twice a week in the gym has to be leading to something tropical for real. So, when my package gets here in about a week or so, I will hang up my red frilly bikini on my closet door and see if that motivates Charlene to be her best self.

**Charlene:** *"Bring it on. I'm redefining the bikini body, one jiggle at a time. Let's do it."*

*Friday, April 13, 2018*

Listen, the gym fashion experience is too much. I have noticed that more and more of the girls are totally dolled up to work out. I mean full falsies, and contouring makeup to go with their Etsy-designed compression leggings and racer tops. These ladies are out performing pirouettes to make their butts look big in their gym wear. How on earth can you run on a treadmill with a wedgie in your butt, and your ass flapping around?

I'm there trying to hold my girls down on my chest and run. I can't hold both my boobs, Charlene, and my ass all at the same time while I run on the treadmill. I feel bad to put the thing on the slightest incline because even the treadmill starts to tremble. Every part of my body is jiggling once I start up that treadmill. Is shaking supposed to help you lose weight? I don't get it at all. Meanwhile, these girls are doing their best to make it all shake with every rep.

The saddest thing is, the guys don't even talk to them. They wait impatiently, complaining about poor form when the girls use the weight machines. It is total man lust in the gym. The women are lusting after the guys, and the guys are lusting after the guys, too. I'd have better luck picking up a muscle man by picking up a *Men's Fitness* magazine.

Speaking of which, my dude, "Mr. Strong", has decided those magazines are a waste of time anyway. The sales guy at GNC told him all he needs to do is drink Muscle Milk, take testosterone, swim twice a week, and he would get totally toned. He's decided all the gym dudes are on 'roids. He convinced himself of a whole new way to get fit without having to set foot in the gym. I better go find out what the magic formula is for women. Because clearly the gym isn't working for me. I haven't lost an inch or a pound. Charlene and I are jiggling away and impressing no one. Not the guys, and yeah, my baggy old t-shirts are not impressing the Pinterest crowd, either.

It wouldn't hurt for Chad to see me in something other than busted t-shirts and old leggings. I want him to see that I'm not a slob and I do care how I look. In fact, I look much better not in workout clothes and puffy and sweaty. Maybe I could go in a little earlier and change at the gym. Perhaps he won't be so mean to me if he saw that I could look good, even with Charlene riding shotgun.

Charlene had an opinion about that train of thought. "*I'm not your flaw, girl, I'm your feature. Dress me up and show me off.*"

I'm going to have to go shopping again, without an unhelpful personal shopper, to get some cute workout clothes. I want to kick my whole image up a notch, and let those Pinterest workout girls see a new me. What is self-love if I can't even love myself enough to dress my body nicely?

I wonder where could I go to find some nicer workout gear. Even in the gym fitness shop, everything in my size is still basic black. I can't even look like a radioactive 80s leotard girl if I wanted. I guess it would be odd to see marshmallow women like myself in neon green and fuchsia pink. But back to the sizing scams: if you want to get bigger sizes, you might need to call in a private detective. They don't even have decent compression tights in my size that aren't transparent, so all I'd be doing is showing off my grapefruit-skin cellulite to the world. I swear it is a conspiracy to keep fat girls out of the gym. Yes, I used the real F word... FAT!

Shouldn't they make gym clothes for the people who need to go to the gym? The shop is only an assortment of bras, shorts and leggings. I guess they assume all women want to work out in bra tops and high-waisted leggings. The bra tops aren't even good quality.

I'm yet to find a decent sports bra that supports without allowing the girls to flop. That spandex sports bra material doesn't help to keep shit down. They smush the girls out flat, and still my breasts manage to slap me in the face while I try to run on the treadmill. I wear an underwire bra under my sports bra in order to keep the girls under control. Similarly, I put on compression tights to keep Charlene contained while I work out. Otherwise, she would be flopping around like a live fish on deck. She keeps trying to do a dramatic jump out of the top of my leggings to get attention. I should not need to wear Spanx to fit into gym clothes.

I did find something in the fitness section of Target that I like and am willing to wear. My new favorite fitness clothes are those cute tennis skorts. Nope, I don't play tennis and I also don't wear them to the gym to work out. I wear them at home to lounge in. They're so easy to wear. Like shorts but they don't advertise that your thighs are going at it hot and heavy, rubbing each other down. They're long enough to cover the worst of the cellulite, but short enough to be cute. I wear them all the time around the house. They are so comfy when it's hot.

Charlene was all in: *"Shimmy in your mini, girl. I like these skorts, too."*

My yoga pants are also not errand clothes nor are they for actual yoga. I haven't found a brand that does not show off my dumplings and cream cheese legs, so it is leggings and tunics for me when I go to the store. But yoga pants at home when it's cold, I can get with that. So, I guess looking sporty-ish is my new casual fashion.

Besides browsing the gym store, I did that super-quick thirty-minute circuit. It might not have accomplished much, but I *was* in the gym. That absolutely counts. I felt accomplished just for showing up for more than my free training sessions.

To celebrate, I had a green chai smoothie. The drink was so sweet that I'm sure it negated all the effort I'd put in. But a girl and her belly have to enjoy something about this gym life.

**Charlene:** *"Bring on the chai smoothies. They're smooth and delicious."*

*Wednesday April 25, 2018*

These past two weeks have been excruciating. After that first session with Chad, his true colors began to show. He had taken it easy with me those early sessions to get me to commit. That was my first mistake. I thought Tanya was a gym freak, but this guy took it to the next level. Chad is a beast. Not only to me but to everyone he trains. I came in early and caught the last fifteen minutes of his session with one of the gym bros. It was brutal. I felt tired and sore only from looking on. My muscles were filing complaints from the sidelines. Then he had him stand on this vibrating plate.

"What's the deal with the weird shaking machine in the gym?" I asked Chad.

"The vibration plate was designed for the space station. It's designed to help build bone density to strengthen and toughen your bones. It activates your core muscles for balance and will help tone as well. Only the best gyms cater to it. If you change to a smaller gym, you won't have the same benefits," he said.

"So, I just have to stand on it, and magically it will make me stronger and more toned. That's my kind of exercise. Just stand there and shimmy. I'm sold. When can I do it?"

"No, it doesn't work just like that. You have to use it after exercise for the benefit," he said.

That made it much less appealing. I guess I don't want to use it after all. More time at the gym is not the answer to any question I have.

As the other guy left drenched in sweat, Chad grinned and said he'd gone light on him. He muttered that the "fella is a tub of lard in the wrong places". Wrong places? Where exactly are the right places? If belly fat counts as a place, Charlene has been living there rent-free for years. Can I evict her and send her to the right spot? Charlene seems to think she's in the prime spot, center stage. She gets the VIP section of my body.

Chad, however, has been trying to kill me with insidious workouts that don't hurt while I do it, but makes me beg my boyfriend for massages the next day. Strangely, the more I exercise, the less it hurts, so the incentives are more messed up. Work out till it hurts and keep working out so it will hurt less. Is this good for me? How does this compute?

I can't decide if the training session was better or worse when Tanya joined me. She came to the gym outfitted in a bright orange sports bra and adorable running shorts, all chic and cute. Naturally, I looked like a sweaty mess in my baggy tee-shirt and old gray leggings. Chad was impressed with Tanya's stamina and fitness as he worked us through his sets.

I was being proved wrong in real time. The gym bros don't notice the fat girls in the gym, but they surely notice the hot girls. All eyes were on Tanya, but she didn't even notice. She was trying to have full-on debates with me in between sets. She was unbothered while I was gasping, grunting and trying to catch my breath.

"We haven't gone to the Neon Watering Hole in months. Did The Dude ban you from singing karaoke or what? You never want to do anything but sit on the couch and cuddle with him," she remarked.

"That's not true. They changed the karaoke to Thursday nights and you told me you couldn't make it. Plus, you never come over for our pizza nights anymore. That used to be our time," I defended.

"How can it be our time if The Dude is always there, lying on your chest. Do you think I want to sit next to y'all snuggled up on the couch? It used to be our time, but now he's always there. It's all about the two of you," Tanya said.

"Do you think the gym is the place for us to have this conversation? Really, right now?"

"When else do I see you anymore? Maybe, this could be our new thing. You need to lose the weight and I want to start lifting. You should stick it out, instead of giving up," she said.

"Hold on, I'm not here to lose weight. You don't get to decide what I need to do... and I hate coming to this smelly gym. I tried to like it, and it was fun for about ten minutes. Not for two whole hours. I'm wired differently to you. You love the gym and that's great. I don't," I said.

"You haven't even tried it. You keep giving up and flaking out," she accused.

"I've been doing this training with Chad for weeks. I've been doing it, even though I hate it. But I'm done with Chad and his sadistic squats as soon as my free sessions are over. The only thing good in here is the chai smoothies," I said.

"So, you won't work out with me? You're quitting on me and the gym?"

"I'm not quitting on you, Tanya. We just have to come up with a different plan. I'm not built for this gym life," I said.

Charlene protested: *"Nope, don't kill my vibes. We need to keep coming to the gym. I'm in love with the vibration machine. I love getting my Shakira on. My hips don't lie; this jiggle will get you in trouble."*

I ended every training session with Chad doing at least fifteen minutes on the vibration plate. I'm sure it doesn't mutate my bones into titanium strength. I swear all eyes are on me when I'm on that thing, which may be why Charlene loves it. Anything that gets the spotlight, she's all for it. She was doing belly dance shimmies like Shakira's hips. I wondered, do I even need to go to the gym for the vibration exercise? I could let my boyfriend play the drums on my tummy. He's always tapping his fingers; might as well let him harness his nervous energy to loosen my fat cells and get toned.

**Charlene:** *"I'll allow The Dude to play, but he has to pay me in cheesecake."*

*Friday, April 27, 2018*

I skipped the gym today. I didn't want to see Tanya or Chad. I hate the feeling that everyone else thinks my body needs fixing. After all this time I have been trying to empathize and see her point of view, she's still ignoring mine. Why am I not enough?

The Dude also complained that I was neglecting him, so we decided to have a personal movie night. As always, he picked some action movie with lots of bombs. I can barely sit through those as the lack of logic irritates me, and he can never explain what's going on with the story anyways. I looked up from my *People* magazine to check out the muscled leading man, and scoffed at his miraculous ability to avoid injury and perform He-Man feats of strength. In tonight's beyond-belief scene, the muscle man lifted up the leading lady like she weighed nothing, and ran away from an erupting volcano. He just scooped her up and did his action hero thing.

I turned to The Dude. "Can you do that to me? Do you think you can lift me if you had to save my life?"

"Well, if I had to, I'd drag you."

Drag me! That was his best possible answer? All that Muscle Milk, all those protein shakes, and he still can't lift me up. What's the point of weightlifting if he isn't getting any stronger?

"Oh, wait, you haven't actually been going to the gym or working out. So, you're right, you can't lift me. If you'd have to drag me, I'd probably have to save myself."

He frowned at my reply.

"I wonder if Chad could lift me. I'd need a super strong man who can lift me up. I need to think bigger than him, even. Maybe The Rock; we need to call The Rock. The Rock would save me. The Rock looks like that, effortless, heroic, larger than life, like he could rescue a woman from a volcano." I meant The Rock part as a joke, but the look on The Dude's face made me realize he wasn't taking my chatter lightly. He could dish it out the mean jokes, but he couldn't take it.

The Dude muttered about an early meeting and left. He didn't even finish watching the silly movie. Guess he didn't like being compared with movie stars.

I didn't like the thought of having to be dragged to safety. I do like the thought of a hero being able to whisk me away to safety. Maybe I do need a muscle man in my corner.

So, I am making my own list. Celebrities who could save Charlene and me:

- The Rock

- Arnold Schwarzenegger

- Sylvester Stallone

- Jason Statham

- Jason Momoa

**Charlene:** *"Girl, let The Dude drag you to safety. But if Jason Momoa shows up, I'd be jumping into his arms like the world is on fire."*

*Monday, May 7, 2018*

I have barely survived another two weeks of gym training, with no more Tanya tag-alongs. She's still using The Dude's membership, but not with me. I don't have two-hour gym stamina. Have you been wondering about my boyfriend's dedicated gym schedule? HAHA.

Since his "flu outbreak" he has not set foot back into the gym.

He is almost out of Muscle Milk. It would seem that he has been trying to get all his gains from drinking protein shakes instead of working out. So, it's now or never time for him. Either he has to return to the gym or admit that the weight machines have defeated him. Will he ever admit he was wrong to convince me to double up on gym membership?

I already know how this is going to go... he will start to roll out the excuses... hey, wasn't I the one who wanted to work out and wasn't I going to cancel the membership? He went to support me, yadda yadda yadda. My favorite bit is when he says he loves me the way that I am and I don't have to change for him; it's up to me. Once I'm happy. Yeah, sure, until we go on a cruise and he wants pictures cozied up to some hot cabaret dancer.

One bright spot has emerged from the last of my gym sessions. I ran into Bella, an acquaintance from college days, in the gym yesterday. I didn't remember her, but she called my name brightly, and started chatting about the guys in engineering. She was a liberal arts major, she explained, and we didn't take any classes together. She used to see me all the time in the engineering quad. I looked at her again and realized she did seem vaguely familiar.

Back when we were in college together, Bella was about the size I am now, but she's shorter than me so she looked much thicker then. She's a much bigger size now. I was surprised to learn that she's a regular gym babe. She doesn't go for the Zumba class. She's into spin and yoga. I took her suggestion to do yoga as I figured it would be less strenuous.

I was wrong, and Bella was absolutely impressive in the class.

I could barely touch my toes and there she was turning into a pretzel and triangle posing the shit out of the place. She's flexible despite her size. Man, do I feel inferior. At the end of the class, I complimented her ability. She reminded me huffily that being fat does not mean not being fit. She assured me that she could run a marathon if she wanted. She has already done a 10K and is planning to start training for the longer distance. I don't have such aspirations, but if she wants it, then go, girl.

She's the case study for proving that big girls can be fitter than skinny ones. I was breathing hard from the yoga warm up stretch, and she smiled breezily through it all.

Charlene commented, "*Why are you looking at her size. You should be admiring her confidence and her personality. She's as bubbly as me.*"

Marcus didn't remember Bella when I mentioned her in the office.

"She wasn't in any classes with me since she was a psychology major. She was always hanging around the engineering quad and I think she was very popular, with the guys anyway," I explained.

"Liberal arts major named Bella. Oh, you mean, the Good Times blimp?" Marcus said.

"Why would you say that about her?" I asked, horrified.

"Hey, that's what they called her, the engineering guys. I never did anything with her. I didn't get with any of the desperate fat ones like her," he said.

"All fat girls are not desperate!" I protested.

"Probably not all, but Bella surely was. Any guy that smiled at her could ride her. I'm telling you, that was the talk," Marcus insisted.

I never paid much attention to others' sexual escapades during college, too caught up in trying to maintain my scholarship and the lab job that took up a lot of time. My time to scope out who was doing whom was pretty limited. Marcus seemed ready to go into detail about who did what and to whom, and honestly, I was disgusted. I cut that topic short. I wasn't going to allow him to slut-shame Bella or any of the other girls we might have known in college. The guys were almost always more desperate than the girls.

Marcus wasn't very active on the social scene in our college days. I remember him being extremely shy. He didn't say anything to me, or any of the other two girls in the C+ programming class until we were assigned in a group project. His idea of a date was probably a two-hour calculus study session in the engineering library. He and Tanya used to study a lot together that year we did the calculus class. She had thought he was cute, but he never made a move on her. I would be surprised if he ever even had a girl in his dorm room.

Maybe he is so offensive about women now because he wasn't so good at talking to them. I think he gets some bragging rights with the other guys for having known me socially. He has gotten too friendly with Greg, who I may have to report to HR again. I swear I heard Greg asking Marcus about my bra size the other day.

**Charlene**: *"Girl, you definitely need to escalate the HR complaints against Greg."*

# *Eight*

## WORKING OUT IS AN OUTER BODY EXPERIENCE

Wednesday, May 9, 2018

Is he jealous?

The Dude came to the gym today after months of recuperating from his shoulder injury and flu. He didn't come with me when I was leaving for my training. Instead, he said, "Don't be surprised if you see me there. After all, we have to use our membership." Yeah. He's been in the gym all of three times since he had me upgrade my hated membership to a group plan. So of course, now he has to use it.

I have been relaying Chad's advice to Dude for weeks. Perhaps he finally heard enough about Chad and wanted to scope him out himself. He did not stay long. He also didn't work out. He didn't even come over to talk to me. Instead, he hovered in the shop area, browsing protein bars and muscle tees.

He was strangely, always conspicuously within my line of sight. I wonder if Chad felt holes burning in his back. Chad came over to help me with my form during one of my sets, and suddenly I heard a crash in that general area. When I could get up and looked over, he was gone. No goodbye, no post-gym hangout.

Charlene figured it out: *"Girl, he's not jealous of Chad. He's jealous of Chad's biceps. And maybe of your attention. Time for another belly dance session."*

I think seeing Chad in the flesh was a bit intimidating. Chad is all muscle and confidence, and The Dude… well, let's just say his pushup form is lacking. He didn't come back to my place after, either. Later, when I texted him, he claimed he went to buy some Muscle Milk and vitamins. Right.

It was a bit much. Was it a reconnaissance mission, or retail therapy disguised as gym attendance? Am I just self-obsessed, or did he come to spy on me? It felt like a lot of energy, glaring in my direction, and why come all the way to the gym to not work out? I'm sure that's not the exercise of the month in *Men's Fitness.*

**Charlene:** *"The Dude is keeping his eyes on me. He doesn't want Chad to mess with perfection."*

*Friday, May 11, 2018*

Marcus was berating Greg in the office for his lame attempts to chat up Lucy. Greg one-upped him by saying at least he talked to a real woman and not a screen. The office went quiet.

Marcus returned to his cubicle. Of course, I had to find out what was going on. As far as I knew, Marcus was single, but there seemed to be some office gossip that missed me. "What's up with that comment, Marcus? Have you been holding out on me?" I asked.

It turned out that he had been chatting up some girl on an online matching site and the guys were teasing him about it. I started in with the third degree.

"Tell me about her. How long have y'all been chatting? What is she like? Have you met her in person yet? Can I see a photo?" I asked. He sheepishly showed me the photos and she was quite beautiful, but seemed so familiar. He was shy about the topic.

"I know I'm not a match for her in looks, so I've been trying to impress her with my personality. She thinks I'm sensitive and understanding," Marcus said.

"That's not going to work, Marcus. That's not who you are. Sensitive, please!" I scoffed.

Then I realized that I recognized her face. His online girlfriend is a model. She's on the product posters in the weight shop in the gym.

"Marcus, I have to break it to you. Whoever you are talking to, that's probably not how she looks. Those photos are from an actual model. A woman like that is not matching with guys on the internet. If it's even a woman at all."

He looked crushed, but not shocked. He probably had already suspected this was too good to be true.

"I'm telling you, Marcus. Search for 'Tight Threads workout gear'."

Sure enough, "his girl's" face stared right back at him. All the sexy photos she'd sent him were product shots. Some had been oddly photoshopped to look less perfect, but it definitely was the same model. His swagger was gone.

Miss Tight Threads did indeed make the clothes look good. She probably was a size two and they had airbrushed and photoshopped her body to utmost perfection. We would all get suckered in by her photos. I would buy the workout clothes to look just like her. Who am I fooling? Like Marcus, I want her body. Well, not exactly like Marcus, but I want *my* body to be like *her* body.

**Charlene:** *"Forget the models. Even their bodies get photoshopped. You don't need another body to obsess over. I'm already more than you can handle."*

*Monday May 13, 2018*

I encountered Bella in the gym again. I was heading toward the smoothie bar, eyeing one of those green concoctions that promises to erase all dietary sins, when I spotted her. I looked at her with fresh eyes, trying to see what others might miss about her. Fat people are often invisible, judged just by their body. Bella looked super put together, and she wasn't wearing black at all. She was dressed in a flounced leopard print tights and tank top combo, and even her sneakers had a tiger print highlight. It was like she was starring in her own fitness fashion show.

"Bella, you always look so fabulous in the gym. I have to know your secret. How do you find colorful workout gear? Where did you get your outfit?" I asked.

Bella laughed.

"I actually made most of it myself. The sneakers I ordered online, and they were my inspiration. For me, looking good is part defense mechanism, part motivation to keep showing up here," she said.

"That makes sense. Most days, I really don't want to come either," I said.

"Yeah, this place... I also have to special-order my bras. I get this style with anti-slouching control bands. Otherwise, the weight causes back pain," she said.

"Oh, I can totally relate to that. I have been looking for some bras with wider shoulder straps and they're impossible to find in stores," I said. She shared the website details with me, and the whole conversation gave me some pause. I complain about finding jeans that won't strangle Charlene, but Bella has to deal with a different level of logistics.

Then I asked the uncomfortable question. The one you know you're not supposed to ask, but sits heavy in your chest anyway. "I hope you don't mind me asking. Don't answer if it bothers you. How did you put on so much weight since college? Is the gym helping?" I asked quietly.

She didn't flinch at my questions. She told me straight: "I have endometriosis, and I'm on a steroid treatment. That's what made the weight pack on. Sometimes the pain with my condition is unbearable, but if I get too big, then my knees start to hurt, too."

"God, that's awful."

"It is. I have to be super careful with my diet and maintain my fitness routine to manage the side effects of the medication. The gym helps, but even with diet and regular exercise, it's an uphill battle. Honestly, the worst part is the stares, and the loud comments from the obnoxious ones," she said.

"It's already a struggle to get here and then to feel like I'm being judged in here too," I agreed.

"Yeah, I feel it and see it. The silent judgment. The eyebrows that rise in surprise, in cynicism, wondering who let the fat girl in. I don't feel comfortable in the gym, but I know I have to keep doing it. I try to ignore them and push through."

I felt my heart squeeze. Even though we don't share the same dress size, we share the same struggle, just in different bodies. Hers is fighting medication and hormones; mine is fighting Charlene's stubborn refusal to abandon me.

Charlene couldn't resist pointing out: *"See? Everybody has their own challenges, their own story. Don't act like I'm the villain. I'm just part of your plotline – and your waistline."*

It is humbling to see everybody has their own war, their own story. Our bodies are just part of our plotlines. Bella's story reminded me that the struggle isn't about the numbers on the scale or the size stitched into a tag. It's about living inside a body that sometimes feels like it has its own agenda. It's about feeling the weight of judgment even when you are trying to improve yourself. The heaviest thing women of all sizes carry around is society's expectation that we fit into the acceptable mold. Somehow, we are all missing that elusive mark.

I sipped my green smoothie and admired Bella's tenacity. She had all the reasons not to be here, but she showed up anyway.

**Charlene**: *"She probably comes for the chai smoothies. It's almost as good as cheesecake."*

*Tuesday, May 21, 2018*

I didn't see Bella in the gym the last couple times I was there. I used to see her every time I went in ... well, the last three times I went to my training sessions with Chad.

I ran into her in the coffee shop today.

"Hey, Bella, how come I haven't seen you in the gym recently? I was so inspired last time when we talked. I was looking out for you," I said.

"Oh girl, we need to sit down for this. There's been a lot going on."

We ordered some iced lattes and got a table by the window.

"I actually had an emotional setback. This guy I was dating, Kyle, well, we broke up."

"Oh no. What happened?" I asked.

"Kyle had a thing for big girls. He told me when we started talking. At first, it felt so perfect. I thought I'd finally found a guy who loved me as I was. We met in the grocery store and we got to talking about different recipes and cooking. He loved cooking for me and watching me eat. He was super supportive. He never pressured me to lose weight or change," she said.

"That sounds so good. What changed?" I asked.

"We didn't even get intimate until a month in. When we did, he wanted me in lingerie and cleavage-baring outfits. He made me feel confident, like he adored my curves. I started loving myself more because of him. I thought he was the one," Bella continued.

"Go on," I encouraged.

"Since I wanted this relationship to go the distance, I wanted to get fitter, a little sexier so I could look better in those outfits he liked. I even figured we could do a sexy couples' photoshoot with him. Then he started getting all cold, especially on the days that I came back from the gym," she said.

"Cold how?" I asked.

"First, he said my gym time was cutting into our time together. Then he stopped cooking for me. If I mentioned the gym, he wouldn't even come over. We went from seeing each other three or four times a week to just a Friday night Netflix date and a couple of phone calls."

"That's rough. Was he going through something?"

"I thought I could fix it, whatever it was. So, I skipped a gym session and surprised him at his apartment. But I was the one surprised. I found Kyle... licking chocolate syrup off the breasts of some other woman. Turns out he'd been cheating on me with some other 'desperate fatty'. He called us desperate fatties." She looked distraught and I had no words.

"He was just using me, saying the right words, but he didn't mean it. Yes, he liked big women, but he liked that it made us easier to manipulate. He didn't care about my real health and happiness. He didn't even care about the other girl," she said.

"That is so incredibly awful. I'm so sorry you're dealing with that."

"I had to take some time away from the gym, too. The gym feels like a humiliation ritual sometimes. I can't deal with toxic gym culture and predatory guys. I don't know who to trust. Who is being honest with me. I had my wild days in college, sleeping with guys just to get their attention. I'm not doing that now. I really want to find my person," she said.

"Oh, Bella, I'm worried about your health, though. Now, I don't like going to the gym either, but I hate to hear you are giving up on what's helping you. Don't let a loser boyfriend mess that up too," I said.

"I know. I know I have to find another outlet. I'm just taking some time," she said.

I was so demoralized for her and for all fat and skinny womanhood. I felt that I should skip the gym too, in solidarity with her. To my mind, it showed how screwed the fitness ideal is for women. There is no out for us. If you're slim, you're not slim enough. Or your boobs and butt aren't big enough. If you're fat, you aren't fat enough. There's no pleasing the world, or yourself, either.

Mr. Strong was all happy about me skipping the gym. I don't think he is into fat girls, even with all his fat jokes and trying to feed me wontons and cheesecake. I do think he's just a little insecure about me being around a bunch of other, fitter guys. He said he didn't want me to start checking out those muscle dudes in the gym. As if I would. I think men go to the gym to check other men out, because they certainly aren't checking out the sweaty fat girls in baggy t-shirts and old leggings.

The whole debacle with Bella and her guy has strangely depressed me, too. I'm even more tired today from not working out than I usually am from the days when I go to the gym.

**Charlene:** *"Girl, let's get into our couch confessional and decompress with chips and salsa. You cannot mold your body to fit the world. You have to decide what's good for you."*

*Friday, May 25, 2018*

Yesterday, my dude and I watched some ad about freezing out fat cells. I'm a data scientist. I would like to determine the effectiveness by a round of testing.

My boyfriend very helpfully suggested that he would be happy to rub ice cubes around my tummy if I count it as foreplay. He was trying to be funny, but I was willing to try. I was thinking of fat loss for sure, but sex is exercise. I thought I was going to get a two-for-one special. He rolled away from me on the couch and said if I want to exercise so badly, I should just go to the gym.

I think he's jealous of my trainer, Chad. I may have quoted Chad a couple dozen times during the last two months while I worked off my free sessions. It's not my fault my boyfriend does the opposite of everything Chad says is good for you. He still drinks 100% whole cow's milk. He will skip breakfast most days and then eat a giant meal at ten a.m. Then he'll skip lunch and eat a dinner big enough for three people at seven. An hour later, the TV is watching him. In spite of all that, he looks leaner than me.

I am here eating oats, drinking water and having salad and six measly nuts every six hours and I won't eat out after six. What do I get for my good behavior? I look bloated, like a snake after a meal. I am gassy and constipated, too. Then if I so much as look in the direction of a cupcake, I gain five pounds. Meanwhile, he is scarfing down milkshakes and barely has a beer keg. Definitely no six pack, but he isn't sporting any sexy French maid apron or whatever. No fair!

My dude smugly said he is very fit. He forgot, I still remember the "gym flu" episode. He launched into a long speech about the benefits of testosterone. He even went for an issue of *Men's Fitness* to quote the article. I stopped listening long ago, as I just imagined the effects of testosterone would have me looking like that app on my phone: "Would you date your opposite sex?" I already have some stubborn chin hairs and pesky whiskers. I don't need testosterone to add any manly features. It will be me and sexy succubus Charlene French belly apron all the way.

Steroids and hormones are a man's game, anyway. Why would anyone invent pills to make you look bigger? What women really want is a magic shrinking concoction. It would be even better if it came looking like a cheesecake iced with "Eat me" like Alice found in Wonderland.

Chad lectured me at every session about the supplements I should be taking. Why are men always trying to get women to take pills? He insisted that I need vitamin B or D injections to boost my metabolism. I hate injections, but I briefly wondered if this was the missing link to jump-start my body, "re-sculpting", as Chad termed it. Of course, the B shots were some extra benefit that cost $50 a shot.

As The Dude mansplained it to me some more, I was already in the Matrix. I was ready to choose the Blue Pill, and let it all end and be back to fitness oblivion.

As for Charlene, after those six intense training sessions, we're still celebrating non-scale victories. There's a pair of jeans I love that can now skim my hips. I don't have to lay out on my bed to put it on. I'm sure my muffin top is getting a little smaller, too. There might be a chance at the next community barbecue I could swallow my pride and don a swimsuit and go into the pool. I usually wear a sundress and insist that I'm not in the mood to swim. I'm usually not feeling to free Charlene to scrutiny. Hey, all those beer guts and man boobs are proudly on display, so why can't sexy Charlene the French belly apron flutter her eyes.

I have been asking boyfriend to call Charlene (and me) "Cherie amour" to honor her role as sexy French belly apron. He is not on board yet. Even if I say, *"Oui, m'sieur"* in my sexy French maid voice. So much for role playing. Apparently, I'm the only one who is supposed to act during sexy role play. He is just supposed to lie there while I try to be sexy. Is that how it's supposed to work? What about Magic Mike? Shouldn't I get a fake Chippendale with an elephant trunk in the bedroom sometime too?

**Charlene**: *"Ma Cherie, when is the next striptease? I'm always ready to shake and shimmy."*

*Saturday, May 26, 2018*

Maybe I need a healthier boyfriend.

I organized a glamping birthday trip for The Dude. It was outdoorsy but still civilized. There was a tent, but with a full bed, electricity, and all the creature comforts. I thought it would be romantic. It would be a weekend for The Dude and me to bond under the stars. We could sip wine by the fire after walking some forest trails. We could pretend we were rugged adventurers without actually having to rough it.

The Dude was not impressed. At all.

"Who did you plan this trip for? Did Chad tell you he like camping? I sure didn't."

He made it clear that this wasn't his idea of a good time. Nature walks? Hard pass. Ziplining? "Absolutely not." Like I'd asked him to jump off a real cliff. Kayaking and mountain biking were declared to be ways to rush toward death. He even asked if I had taken an insurance policy out on him before dragging him into the wilderness.

The outdoor adventure trip had been a suggestion from Tanya. She had been encouraging me on my health journey when I complained again about how I hated going to the gym. She suggested that there were other ways to have fun moving and doing exercise. Maybe trail walking, hiking and getting out would be a good fit for me. I didn't want to commit to her twice-weekly, snobby, fat-phobic dance class or the gym Zumba, so I decided to try some other options. It had sounded great. Plus, I would get The Dude involved and it could be our couples' thing. Unfortunately, I did not discuss it with him beforehand.

Charlene figured: "*Girl, you wanted the tent, the stars, and the whole romance fantasy. Tanya probably wanted you to do a girls' trip with* her."

He reminded me that he had been cool with Vegas and was on board with the cruise idea. Why didn't I stick with those suggestions? Why did I lure him into the wild, where according to him, he could be mauled by a bear?

The only thing he liked? The fancy steaks they roasted in the main clubhouse every night. We ate dinner out on the open deck, lit only by small citronella candles. He was practically kissing the ribeye while I was trying to point out the constellations. Apparently, the only way to his heart is food. He wasn't interested in any other kind of adventure with me; not the adventure I imagined.

I had hoped we would reconnect, just the two of us, and we could really be partners in something besides food. We're becoming couch potatoes who sleep in front of the TV and we will only get fatter if we keep up this lifestyle.

**Charlene:** "*Don't blame The Dude. He wanted the steak, and you can't make a bear-wrestler out of a steak-lover.*"

Sunday, May 27, 2018

So, I got back home, tired out from the trip that wasn't good. Honestly, I felt more drained than refreshed. Mr. Strong continued to sulk about wasted weekends, bears and zip lines. He hadn't done any of that. Instead, he hung out in the main clubhouse and smoked cigars.

When I mentioned I had to pack my stuff for the gym session tomorrow, he pre-empted me, saying he didn't want to know what else Chad had to say about anything. I reminded him this was my last session. My time with Chad was going to be up, and I, for one, was glad it was over.

When I announced that if I never saw Chad again it would be too soon, The Dude was suddenly all happy again. He wanted to go out to celebrate, but I was not in the mood for Chinese buffet. He didn't even mind. Instead, he even offered to give me a massage. Of course, he also suggested that I could pay him back in cake. Once again, it was not about me. It was about food. Is food the price of love?

Anyways, I decided to bake. I found a red velvet recipe and whipped out the mixer. I told him it was a birthday do over, a chance to reset after the wilderness fiasco.

You know what? That went well. He was happy, I was happy. Charlene was also practically purring with satisfaction. She had been deprived of excess sugar over the weekend, too. We can't have that. We're all a match here; just add cake and everybody wins. Except my red bikini.

**Charlene**: *"See? Forget the bears, forget the tents. Let us eat cake and savor the crumbs."*

*Nine*

## HOTTIES HOOKING UP
## WITH HOTTIES

*Monday, May 28, 2018*

I guess I am not a girl's girl.

Lucy and I were chatting over lunch and I asked her if she was team bikini or team whole suit. I was still working up the nerve to wear the bikini that I had ordered and was still watching hanging on my closet. I had never even tried it on since I received it.

"Oh, I'm absolutely team bikini; the smaller the better. Don't worry, you don't have to copy me, but you should definitely try skinny dipping sometime. Sometimes it is the clothes that trap us. You have to let it all go. It is so freeing to release all your inhibitions. I even did a boudoir shoot for my birthday last year. I went completely nude and the photos were so amazing. If you want to be body positive, that's what you should do." Lucy was off and rambling, talking about the nude beaches in St Maarten and how she couldn't wait to do a full Caribbean cruise.

Now, Lucy, with her on-and-off Caribbean accent and her wild fashions, provides peak entertainment to those IT and maintenance dudes in our building. They chat her up and have her thinking she's the hottest female to walk our halls. She's always on point with fashion trends, with the loudest lipstick, biggest eyebrows and feather earrings or green mohawks or whatever is on *FashionBombDaily*'s happening page. This week, she was sporting unicorn hair for a more avantgarde look on the recommendation of her friend, Michael.

"Is Michael your boyfriend? You mention him all the time." I should have asked before, because she has quoted this guy as the keeper of fashion to me so many times, yet I don't know much about him.

"Well, no, not really. I'm not really into guys like that, you know. And Michael, he's a special friend, but not a boyfriend."

She and Michael apparently have a "girlfriendship", not a relationship, not a situationship. Michael was her stylistic best friend and they hit it off shopping together. They actually met in the mall in the lingerie section of Macy's. That right there was a red flag. Men shopping in that particular area are either shopping for a girlfriend or they aren't playing on the usual team.

He denied to her that he was homosexual, or into drag. Yet, after about six months of "being just friends" he had to gently break up with her because his current partner, who it turns out was male, was getting jealous of their closeness. Lucy couldn't understand why Michael wouldn't make time for her, since their relationship was platonic.

"If The Dude had a female friend that wanted a lot of his time and attention, I would be very concerned. I can see where Michael and his partner might need to draw the line."

That was not what Lucy wanted to hear.

"Not all relationships are about sex," she shrieked at me.

She was completely angry at Michael, and me, apparently, for not standing up for their friendship.

"Why are you taking his side? You should be on my side, knowing that it was platonic. Why are you so insecure about me around your male friends?"

**Charlene**: *"Maybe she was hangry. You should have offered cake. I don't even think this conversation was about you."*

The Dude brought me cheesecake today. It was delicious, but I suspect his motives.

Yesterday, I was celebrating an actual scale victory. I may have officially lost ten pounds from all my gym work, or from not eating carbs after six, as Chad recommended. It could be because I have scaled back on my carbs overall and am doing smaller portions, too. I'm trying to be holistic and make the healthiest choices. The best part is, since I'm drinking a ton more water, I'm feeling less bloated. Charlene's still around, having endured all the planks, crunches and green juice cleanses... but I'm aiming for calm acceptance mode, mostly.

Anyways, my always supportive boyfriend said, "That's great. It was probably water weight, though."

Isn't he always there with a kind and uplifting thought for me? I grumbled that he just didn't know how to celebrate my small wins. My comment spurred him to be more celebratory. So today he brought me something fattening. I have to say, I love cheesecake, but I don't think I'm supposed to celebrate weight loss with food. I can't think of any other way I would want to celebrate, but still, there's a principle there.

Now, don't think that because I lost weight Charlene went anywhere. Nope. I think I may have lost all the weight from my breasts. I have a favorite bra set. It is orange and hot pink lace, like Ms. Fields would have suggested. I bought it ages ago when I was a C cup, so I acknowledge it's no longer my size. It's too pretty to get rid of, plus the matching boy shorts still fit. Well, the bra now fits great again, so this is a true non-scale victory.

Still, if I had to ASK the universe, I would have preferred to keep my D cups and lose all the inches from my belly. I'm not planning eight more training sessions to end up with a flat chest and STILL have a big belly. How can that possibly be incentive to work out?

I still have a pair of jeans that I want to be able to button without having to lie down on my bed and take shallow breaths. That will be the next target to fit into. And well, there are still a couple of dresses in the back of my closet that are haunting me. Do I need to hang those on the closet door too, next to the bikini that is taunting me? I did look at it and imagine myself in it. I like to imagine my outfits before I put them on, but I still haven't gotten the courage to try it yet. I don't want to be disappointed when I look at my reflection in the mirror. Keeping the mental picture intact works for me as a goal.

Is it bad that I want to celebrate my small weight loss victory with a nice lunch out? Such things are best pondered while eating delicious strawberry cheesecake. It was already there, so I had to eat it.

**Charlene**: *"Yes, let's try on the bikini. That should be the reward and then we can celebrate with the cheesecake. Yummy."*

Sunday, June 3, 2018

I met up with Tanya again at the coffee shop. It's the damn carrot cake muffins that keep me going there. She asked me if I ever considered plastic surgery. I don't think we need to mess so directly with our bodies unless there was a medical need, like life threatening or messing with our quality of life. Why would I risk my life and limb to look better? Wait, was she suggesting that I needed surgery?

"Don't get defensive. It's not about you. It's me. This guy I'm talking to… he was saying that there are always options, you know. He said I should think about it." What does she have to think about? Tanya is hot. She's fit and slim and perfect.

She met this guy Justin about a month ago in the mall food court. They have been almost a couple for about two weeks. Apparently, Justin loved that she doesn't have a complex about eating. That's what attracted him to Tanya. She goes to town on a humongous burger and doesn't have an extra ounce of fat. She just has magic metabolism.

"It's my breasts. Justin keeps commenting that I should get a boob job. What do you think?" asked Tanya.

"Girl, take my boobs. I want to be able to eat anything I want and not worry about it. I would also love to shop in the mall and know for sure they have my size. Don't you wish sometimes we could swap out our problem parts?" I was joking as always, but Tanya was truly considering the surgery idea. Justin had told her she should think about cosmetic surgery, a breast augmentation. That's all she needs to be perfect.

"WHAT? No, Tanya, you don't need to mess with surgery. You are so beautiful. You don't want the backache and the trouble to find good bras. Trust me. You should work with what you have. Don't let these guys make you second guess yourself," I said.

What is with these guys trying to police women's bodies? Why do they always feel entitled to comment on our imperfections?

I was surprised he was already ready to talk about that, too. They had only been out together about three times. They weren't even a real couple yet. The sad thing is, his comments play right into Tanya's own insecurities. She didn't need him to take that drill into her sore spot. She has more spirit than me, though. She told him he could keep his thoughts to himself. Of course, she decided to end things with that creep.

She recommitted to the gym. She was thinking to change her strategy, to go for the "bulk and sculpt" approach. There are exercises to increase your butt, work on pectoral definition and work on gaining some mass. She was losing me when she got into the details. I absently mentioned that maybe she would be better set dating a trainer like Chad, someone who would probably appreciate a leaner body type. Plus, Tanya already likes working out and going to the gym. It seems like they would be a perfect match. I even told her so.

I have already figured out I'm not going to be a gym regular, but I can report another non-scale victory!! I did two 30-minute circuits on my own since my sessions with Chad ended. Chad tried to sell me on keeping a training schedule with him. However, I'm not going to pay more for training on top of the gym subscription that I'm yet to figure out the magic formula to cancel.

No, I cannot just go to the membership desk. You have to call the special corporate number at the right moon rising and speak to the membership gods to get that subscription removed. I tried a couple times, but every month that fee keeps showing up on my credit card bill. Where is the 1-800-GOT-GYMS number for the class action lawsuit about contagious sweat and predatory gym subscriptions? Surely subjecting me to the smell of damp towels and body odor fog could qualify me for emotional distress damages. I might have a case and money to claim.

**Charlene**: *"If you win your case, shall we spend our winnings on a vibrating machine, a bread machine and more cheesecake? Please."*

*Tuesday, June 5, 2018*

Am I a mean girl?

I considered that I was being too dismissive about Lucy's issues, so I decided to be nicer. She is my lunch buddy, after all, and has been with me getting all those healthy salads and giving me (somewhat bad) fashion advice. So today, I was extra friendly and encouraging. I complimented her head wrap and batik wrap skirt before we went to lunch. I asked where she learned to tie the wrap in the ethnic style. I was actually curious if it was an island thing, because I thought that was an African style. I was trying to be open and curious.

She got all weird and defensive asking why I was cross-questioning her. She accused me of trying to hit on her, or copy her. Well, I might have been trying to emulate Lucy by wearing more colorful looks and feminine choices. I did follow her advice (and Ms. Fields' suggestions) to get more stylish and not only wear beige or black. Despite me trying to step up my fashion game, I could never be as daring as Lucy. Honestly, I couldn't. My curves would get pulled over by the fashion police. More skirts and more colorful tops are all I tried. My wardrobe doesn't have any ethnic pieces and even my household accessories are beige neutrals. Ms. Fields told me I was a spring, not a summer, which is Lucy's fashion palette.

Lucy insisted that even if I lose weight and tried dressing like her, I would not look better than her. I wondered if I'm such a grump usually that being nice and conversational about fashion with Lucy was freaking her out.

Finally, she came out and explained the reason for her discomfort.

"Why have you been gatekeeping the coding boys from me? Greg told me that you want all their attention, even though he's made it clear that he is interested in me, not you. Why haven't you passed on his invite to their after-work socials?" she asked.

"Why would I be gate keeping those guys from you? Greg is an ass, by the way. I wouldn't inflict him on you," I said.

"He told me you would try to keep me away from him. I know you kept wearing those tight shirts to attract him. He doesn't even want you. Just make sure to pass on his invites next time. I can't access the server room without a pass, and I'm not supposed to leave the desk unattended." Lucy was genuinely mad at me.

"What invite was I supposed to pass on? I don't even go to the socials most of the time. I have a boyfriend already and I'm not interested in any of those guys. If you are into Greg, good luck to you. I'm not at all interested in him," I told her.

"Well, that's what Greg told me. You are always trying to get his attention, and now you're dressing like me too, to get his attention back on you. Greg and I are going to dinner tonight. So now you know, we are dating. It's official," she said.

I was so confused. She looked smug over the announcement. I was never in any competition with Lucy and definitely not over Greg.

"Well anyways, we probably won't be having lunch together as I will be with Greg." Lucy flounced away with those closing words and I was so taken aback. Now I'm replaying all our interactions wondering, where did I misstep with her? Women can't even be friends. We're enemies, frenemies, or plain competition.

**Charlene**: *"Greg is like a virus in the system and she caught it. Guess, she thinks of me as competition, too. My shine is too bright."*

*Friday, June 8, 2018*

Waw! I was totally wrong about the gym. Tanya and Chad are now dating. She held on to my dude's pass and went to work out without me. I was holding her back because I never want to go as hard as she does. Tanya is now absolutely focused on circuit training and learning proper form for curls with Chad.

Also, despite my observation that guys don't notice the girls in the gym, it turns out girls and guys can hook up in the gym. We already knew Chad is a total fitness freak like she is. To be fair, he is a total hunk, too. In fact, he could be the poster boy for *GQ* and *Men's Fitness*. He is easy on the eyes, and is the kind of guy that makes a girl want to train for marathons and put on sexy matching gym wear and crop tops.

I never thought about why she was single for so long, but I'm so glad that she's finding some happiness. I'm good so long as I don't have to be the training buddy anymore. I can't be her accountability partner, because I don't want to be accountable for going to the gym. Plus, she's wearing crop tops and fancy compression leggings. I would look like the dowdy fat girl next to her in my old tights and tee-shirt combo. I would be the ugly best friend that the guys joke about who gets the short straw. I would rather be invisible than be that stereotype. So, I slinked into Zumba and let the beat distract me from the fact that I'm working out on my own now. I'm the only one going to the gym on a group gym membership after I wanted to CANCEL my damn membership plan.

Is it a non-scale victory that I bothered to make it to the gym at all, on my own? I say yes. I haven't actually made it this week yet, but I meant to go. So, it is an almost-victory.

**Charlene**: *"Do we celebrate this victory with cake or ice cream, or both?"*

*Wednesday, June 13, 2018*

Damn, that Chad is slick. He had gotten Tanya on his gym membership, so they were seeing each other three times a week. And all he has to buy is a post-workout protein shake or a green smoothie.

The odd thing is that she said Chad never wanted to go out. Usually, guys want to show off when they have hooked up with a hot girl, so they are ready to go with her to the supermarket just to be seen with her. Yet, Tanya said they only meet at the gym and hang out there. If she wanted to do more, he would go to her place to chill. Their whole relationship revolves around the gym. He always has to work whenever she wants him to hang out.

The Dude was pretty relieved to hear that Chad was going out with Tanya. He actually suggested we make another cameo appearance in the gym.

"You could work out with Tanya and I could do some weights with Chad," he said.

I really didn't want to go to the gym. My training sessions with Chad are done, and I felt like I got my money's worth. I was done with the gym, for real this time. Then The Dude said he was supporting my fitness. Since I was still complaining about having to pay for a group membership that I did not want and WE did not use, we should use it. So, we went.

This time he skipped all the floor weights and stayed on the treadmill the whole time. I did the quick thirty-minute circuit Chad showed me and when I was done, The Dude claimed that he was all caught up in a basketball game on the TV and was ready to go. I didn't protest, just agreed, and was glad to enjoy the drive home without a *Men's Fitness* lecture. I did get a full review of all the bad calls the referee made in the first half, though. When it comes to gym workouts, The Dude is as supportive as a strapless bra. He was really into it and doing the job for the first thirty minutes, then it's all downhill from there.

All in all, I have made it to the gym twenty times in the past three months. I think I have finally gotten some value out of my subscription and can now cancel without guilt. I'm wondering if my credit card will expire this year so they can't auto-renew me. Maybe that is why this whole gym subscription thing went on so long. I missed the cancel window by a day and some clause in the fine print keeps penalizing me.

Besides, my boyfriend now wants to buy a home gym so he can follow the latest *Men's Fitness* program. I have agreed to an exercise bike. I think I can stay committed to my 30-minute workout, especially if it doesn't involve an hour-long road trip. Plus, I think sitting and watching the TV while I exercise could work.

Meanwhile, Tanya officially bought her own membership now, instead of using Chad's or mine. She was pushing for her and Chad to meet up for lunch, and he said that he felt that she was using him for gym access. To prove that was not the case, she decided to get her own membership. While I'm figuring out how to achieve my gym freedom, she got locked down into a one-year contract.

In the meantime, she and Chad are supposed to do lunch this week. I think.

**Charlene**: *"Girl, this last gym outing was The Dude wanting to let Chad see you have a man. He was marking his territory. I like it. Your man has your back. Also, thanks for the chai smoothie."*

*Saturday, June 23, 2018*

Oh damn... I just saw my trainer, Chad, Tanya's man, with some pregnant woman. He was totally looking all up in that face with googly eyes, publicly kissing her and everything that says "this is my woman". How can I unsee this devastation? What am I supposed to do?

I always get the worst news when I stop here at this coffee shop. A carrot cake muffin and a Grande Frappuccino aren't worth the blow to my mental health, or the mental anguish of my friends. I'm here writing in my journal to pretend that I'm not totally scoping out this scene. What do I do? Do I tell her, or maybe this is his sister or ...?

Nope... what brother rubs his sister's pregnant stomach in public. Shit, she's wearing a wedding ring! He's not, but could he be married to her? Is he having an affair with a married, pregnant woman? Who cheats on a girlfriend with a pregnant married woman? I'm so confused and disappointed for Tanya.

At least, I can honestly say that I did not set the two of them up. Though I guess I got her going to the gym where they met. I'm going to get blamed for this no matter how it works out. All because I'm trying to love myself and my belly.

Charlene had some good advice. *"You should take the muffins to go. Savor them home in the comfort of the couch. This coffee shop is always the scene of some drama. You should also call your friend and spill this news."*

I called Tanya and started asking some pointed questions. I was trying to find a good way to let her know that all was not right with her gym hookup. I couldn't come right out and say it.

I tried to be cool and ask her what she knows about him. Did they ever meet up for lunch, and how the relationship is going stuff. She said it's all cool but he hasn't let her come over to his place at all. They don't talk in the night, ever... and most of their dates are before or after going to the gym. He checks her at her place and they don't go out at all. Seeing as they are already out together in the gym, she hadn't thought that much of it... but they get there separately and leave separately. It's a gym and hookup relationship, to be honest.

She might already be starting to figure it out. Tanya must be the outside woman to the woman in the coffee shop. I absolutely don't want to say anything about what I saw because the messenger is always the guilty one.

I gently suggested that maybe she needed to push the boundaries of the relationship a bit so that it could 'develop'.... What I wanted to tell her was don't let homeboy use you. If he won't see you in public, it's because you are the side chick. I bit my tongue and when she suggested an after-gym coffee.

Charlene wasn't sure she agreed with me. *"Girl, I know you don't want to be the bearer of bad news. They always blame the messenger, but you have to let her know the truth."*

I had tried to tell Lucy the truth about Greg and she thought I wanted him for myself. Will Tanya think I want Chad, too? He was my trainer and I definitely saw more of him than I wanted. If I was interested, I'd still be in the gym sweating with him. This is agonizing.

I finally texted her this message.

**<T, you need to call Chad and ask him what his relationship status is. I just saw him out with someone else and it didn't look platonic.>**

It took her a while to respond but I finally got a text back.

<I've reached out but he's not answering. Are you sure it was him?>

I replied.

<T, I'm sure. It looked really bad.>

**Charlene:** "*We had to let her know. She got taken in by Chad's washboard abs, but his heart is the muscle that needs working out.*"

Oh dear. She called him. She didn't get on to him until very late, but he didn't lie to her. She asked him why he wasn't answering her calls and why they can't go out to dinner to talk. He straight up told her that he's not ready to leave his wife yet!!! His wife!!! His pregnant wife!!! Tanya was dumbstruck.

Apparently, Chad has an issue with fat people, and he's been finding it hard to be intimate with his wife while she's pregnant. He decided to get a stand-in until the baby comes. He told Tanya that if his wife's body doesn't bounce back after the baby, then they might have a shot at something long-term. He declared he can't deal with fat chicks, and his wife knows that. She used to be a cheerleader but she's letting herself go with this pregnancy (his words).

How can a guy be so callous to talk about his wife that way? Tanya is more angry than heartbroken. The relationship was too new for her to be too invested. I may be angrier than her. I'm so, so angry at him for being such a sleaze and a douche. Like women don't have enough to deal with, to also have to worry about your husband's feelings when you gain baby fat. How can he cheat on the woman carrying his child! She's the one who is doing the most, surrendering her whole body to create the family, and he's there doing the most to screw the whole thing up. I was in "man is evil" mode when I got off the phone with Tanya.

My dude couldn't even look at me because I was spitting fire on all men. I'm so mad at that disgusting specimen and so angry on behalf of Tanya, Chad's wife and even Charlene. We don't exist to be disposable eye candy for disgusting men like that. AAARRGGHHHH!!!!

Also, if I hadn't already been determined to do so, I totally would quit that gym out of solidarity with Tanya. It isn't fair to be sweating like a pig for the benefit of men like that. It's not worth it.

Tanya, however, has refused to quit. Plus, she's locked into that year contract. She said she's going to keep working out and making sure Chad sees what he is missing. I think that seeing what he is missing is part of Chad's real problem. She didn't join the gym for him and she's not dropping it for him, either.

Maybe the dance troupe diss is still burning her, too. I don't even think Chad fazed her all that much. It may have reinforced her need to stay fit and get fitter. Whatever her motivation, Tanya is officially a gym freak. She's talking about starting a fitness blog.

**Charlene**: *"I support you locking off the gym and Chad. We don't need that negativity in our life. We'll have to find a new source for chai smoothies."*

*Ten*

# EVERYBODY LOVES SOME KIND OF BODY

*Tuesday, July 3, 2018*

I need to do something to cheer Marcus up.

Yesterday, there was some kind of altercation at his football game, and today he was just off. He was being strange and withdrawn. I thought maybe he was still embarrassed about the fake model girlfriend fiasco, but no, this was heavier. He told me he didn't even confront the person. He just cold turkey stopped chatting with them.

It was Greg who spilled the beans about what's really going on. Apparently, Marcus got into a shoving match with one of the maintenance guys who kept nagging him about his online girlfriend. The guy shoved him and Marcus fell down. Marcus got up angry, barreled into him, but then got shoved down again and pinned. Twice. That's the part that is messing with his psyche. He is feeling weak, demoralized, like he's lost his man badge. Now he thinks he needs to bulk up, hit the weights, and get stronger so no one can push him around again.

He imagines that getting bulky and strong will make him more attractive to women, too. Right now, the muscle man physique couldn't be less appealing to me. I think Chad's smarminess has taken the luster off that type. I know it's not all gym bros, but right now he's the gym bro I loathe.

I don't know what to say to him. I can't encourage anyone to go to the gym when I am actively trying to avoid it myself. If I thought he really needed the gym to build his morale and strength, I would tell him to go for it. However, I think the gym bro lifestyle is just another way to make people feel inadequate in their bodies. So, I said nothing.

I'm stuck between empathy and silence. I want to cheer him up, but I don't think the answer is in weights or reps. Strength is more than just about muscles. Attraction isn't based on how much you can lift. The real knocks aren't even the physical. I think it's the online fakery that has hit him the hardest. Besides, Marcus didn't tell me any of this himself. If he wanted me to know, he'd have told me. He probably would prefer I didn't know, to protect his ego.

**Charlene:** *"Girl, you're not his fitness coach. But you could donate The Dude's left-over protein shakes to him. Just saying."*

*Saturday, July 7, 2018*

Did I mention that The Dude bought me some fitness equipment? Except *he* didn't buy it. He used my credit card because he was watching some late-night informercial at my place. The ones that go on for about an hour about how this equipment is going to revolutionize health and re-grow bones and organs. He actually called an 800-number and gave these people my credit card information. He had the audacity to say it was a reward for all my effort in the gym and he didn't want me to give up on my health.

I can't decide if he is being sweet or obnoxious in saying I need to keep working out, both at home and at the gym. He didn't like me interacting with Chad, the cheating trainer, so he wanted me working out at home. That showed some concern. But that means he still thinks I need to lose weight. That's insulting, isn't it? Plus, he used MY MONEY to buy me a gift.

I forgot the worst part. He also got himself "Perfect Pushups" and even bought me some Beach Body fitness pack. I received his three a.m. impulse purchase about two weeks ago and those pushup circles are already dusty.

Surprisingly, I'm loving the Beach Body DVD. The music is fun and it's not as intense as Zumba, but Shaun T is HOT. I've found another gym bro who is easy on the eyes. There are a lot of hips shaking and gyrating, and I learned in the gym that shaking fat cells makes me toned and stronger. Charlene loves all hip-shaking exercises. And, Shaun T makes me want to shimmy sexy French Charlene in his direction.

Also, Bella sent me an invite to start training for a marathon with her. She said she is not going to the gym anymore. She told me she found the gym culture was toxic and had negatively affected her mental health. Although she was clearly fit and able to do a lot of the classes, she still got so many weird looks and comments about the gym not working for her.

Instead, she has formed a trail runners group called "Fat Girls Run". She met some like-minded ladies who are avid runners and although they don't fit the stereotype, they love running 10Ks. So, she's going after her marathon goal and not letting the gym guys or girls keep her back. She graciously invited me to join her group and while yes, I'm still fat, I am not in the running category. I'm happy for her, but nope, I won't be doing any marathons, either.

Do you know the first guy who ran a marathon – back in Greece or whatever, died at the end of it? Seems like a message to me.

**Charlene**: *"That dude took running till you drop too literally. You don't have to run, or hike or gym hard. I say we focus on just dancing for Shaun T and The Dude."*

*Sunday, July 8, 2018*

Tanya has started her fitness blog on Instagram and it is starting to do well.

In her earliest posts, she called out the stupid dance troupe but then said it inspired her to take her health and wellness more seriously. I even got a little spotlight as she used a couple of the audition photos in the intro spot to some of her posts. She's using them as her "before" photos though, as a reference for how much more toned she is. If I'm being honest, I still think she looked perfect before this whole quest for "cut and definition".

She's aspiring to participate in a bodybuilding event, not in the muscle part but in the wellness part. Apparently, there are different categories for women, even a bikini one. Who knew?

I was explaining all this to The Dude and mentioning how the Instagram influencer lifestyle seems to be quite motivating for Tanya. I told him I support her page but the gym life is not my calling. I was just going to enjoy the Beach Body DVDs with Shaun T that he so "lovingly" ordered for me.

Not to be cowed, The Dude proved to be determined to spoil my fun. He proceeded to show me Shaun's Instagram. Turns out Shaun is a happy gay man with twins, and is a proper family man with an equally handsome hunky man as his partner. Double the HOT!!!

That's not what boyfriend wanted me to notice, but the heart sees what it wants. I am happy for Shaun and his family and I will still shimmy my fat for him. When a man looks that good and has such great dance moves, I will keep on trying to catch his eye.

The real reason why women have so many gay best friends is because we secretly want to be the one that converts them. Or maybe because we feel safer with them. We know they aren't going to manipulate us into a relationship or sex. Or maybe it's because they tell you honestly what looks good on you. Aha! I needed a gay image consultant. Maybe I need Shaun T as my personal trainer and wardrobe consultant.

There must be something in the sauce we can give him. Didn't I say Charlene was a sexy French maid succubus? I can get Shaun T's attention somehow. I will keep at it.

**Charlene**: *"I am all about dancing. Girl, let's jiggle and wiggle."*

*Sunday, July 22, 2018*

Tanya has some audacity. She actually asked me to pose for her "Fitstagram" page so she could demonstrate some exercises. She wants me to think of it as my "before" stage. I am not her fitness project. She thinks she is being my friend, but I'm not hearing that.

Somehow, we keep having the same conversations. It is the same conversation I am having with myself in my head, but it just feels so much more insulting when other people tell you the thoughts you've been having yourself.

I know I'm fat. No one else needs to tell me that.

I deflected as I always do: "No one wants to see a chunky monkey as their fitness guru," and we laughed. Laughter does cover a multitude of tears.

Charlene prodded at my conscience, *"Tell her how you really feel. She needs to lay off trying to fix us."* I mustered up my courage. This was my bestie. I used to feel I could tell her anything.

"Actually, Tanya, I'd appreciate if you stop making suggestions like you think my weight is a project for us to work on. I'm committed to being healthy, but I don't need constant reminders about what I should be doing. This is not my 'before' body. This is my body, and it's not up to you to decide if this is how it stays," I said.

Tanya snapped up from her phone. My tone must have alerted her that the time for jokes was over.

"Well, but… I didn't mean… I mean… you know, we always joke about it. I was only trying to help. I'm sorry." She couldn't quite get her words out.

"Charlene isn't going anywhere. Come on, you've seen me three dress sizes smaller. This is my body shape. I'm also not going on Instagram to show it off to the whole world. That's your stage. You can keep the spotlight." I smiled to let her know that I wasn't being mean. This was my boundary.

To totally change me as the subject, I recommended that she check with Marcus. He mentioned that he wanted to start training and bulking up. Maybe Tanya could get him started and they could work on whatever fitness idea she had in mind with him.

"That's great. Get some male perspective, too. Oh, that's such a good idea. Thanks."

She seemed pretty excited to call him, and I was reminded that they did study together a lot when we were in college. Maybe they need to reconnect and help each other out. It could be a match made outside of the gym. As obnoxious as Marcus can be, he did look out for me when I fainted and he truly does keep the worst of the jerks in the office from being such cavemen. He has some redeeming qualities and maybe Tanya can find some more if she looks closely.

**Charlene**: *"Go you, telling your friend to mind your boundaries. I see a shiny backbone back there."*

*Thursday, August 16, 2018*

Charlene is my exercise wing-woman.

I keep trying to get the boyfriend to support me in no-gym movement. I've suggested a dance class, something fun with music we could both enjoy. I've floated the idea of swimming, tennis, or maybe a little weekend badminton. He said he's allergic to exercise. Allergic! As if sweat is pollen and cardio is a bee sting.

Charlene and I nodded along at him while snacking on some trail mix. I think this granola and nuts thing is supposed to be heart healthy, lower my cholesterol and cause me to levitate. Whatever else it does, it tastes good.

He reminded me about the muscle he pulled in the gym months ago. He insisted that it still hurts. That one injury has become his permanent hall pass to be a couch potato. He even pointed out that he bought me fitness equipment. We don't need to go to the gym. I could work out and he could cheer me on in the same room. I noted that his Perfect Pushups are still dusty.

So, I guess we are not the couple that works out together. The dream of us as a sporty power couple is just that, a dream. I'm not going to negotiate exercise with him if it feels like a hostage situation. Maybe he is more in tune with his body and if he likes himself as is, who am I to judge? Okay, I judge, I know. I will try to be more accepting.

His answer to everything I ask is, what do I want to eat? Is he one of those food fetish guys, or is he actively trying to sabotage my healthy living and belly reducing efforts? I'm trying to work with him, but he's not trying to work with me.

So instead, the reality will be me, Charlene and an upbeat playlist. She's along for the ride anyways and these days, she jiggles to the beat.

**Charlene:** *"Girl, he's not allergic to exercise, he's allergic to effort. Stop trying to drag him into our movement. I'll jiggle along with you. We'll be the duo that moves, and get our belly dance on."*

*Wednesday, August 22, 2018*

I am finally free of the gym!

Despite my multiple requests for corporate to release me from this bondage, I finally figured out the magic unsubscribe code myself. I decided to release myself from the credit card gym subscription carousel.

Strangely, it was all the drama with The Dude's offensive gym equipment that prompted me to it. He might have done me a favor. After his late-night gym equipment purchase landed on my credit card, I noticed I had multiple recurring subscriptions on my bill. Some of them I couldn't even remember what they concerned. This particular card was the keeper of all my unwanted and forgotten services, and I needed to take back my control. I canceled the card, reasoning that no one can charge a card that no longer exists. This, my jolly journal, was the secret sauce!

Now that I have a new credit card number, the gym and all my secret subscriptions can't keep charging me for services I don't want, don't use, and can't be bothered to work out the cryptic "unjoin" handshakes.

I got a letter from the gym indicating that my membership was terminated for failing to keep a current card active on file. Of course, I was informed that I was welcome to come in to update my information and my membership would be renewed. I never laughed so hard at junk mail.

In case you're wondering, the offending home gym equipment is now a clothes rack in my bedroom. It may have been used by The Dude once to prove that he is capable of putting things together. The Shaun T DVD still gets an occasional watch. My excitement about jumping around my living room has waned, but The Dude has mentioned that he wants to try Shaun T's Insanity 20 DVD extreme workout program. The name alone tells me all I need to know about that workout. I'm not insane and I'm not falling for it.

Also, The Dude no longer has credit card privileges, so if he buys that incredibly expensive set of DVDs, it will absolutely not be on my dime. It might end up in my DVD player, since he has been stretched out on my couch more afternoons this week than in his place. I'm not complaining. He has continued to apologize for his misstep with donations of Chinese food and cheesecake. So in spite of his failings, I continue to believe he loves me ... and Charlene, by extension.

I guess that means I'm keeping him for now. He's like my comfy period underwear... whether I'm bloated or distressed, he's the only thing that gets me, Charlene and all.

**Charlene**: *"Did you say The Dude brought cheesecake? I forgive him, but we need a better apology, and three more deliveries just like this. Make him sweat."*

*Saturday, August 24, 2018*

Lucy gave me the idea and I went for it. I booked a boudoir shoot. Not a naked shoot; let's not get ahead of ourselves. It was a sexy lingerie shoot. I was confident enough to role play for The Dude. Why not do it for myself? I packed my French maid outfit, including the pink wig. But the real test was my red bikini. That thing had been haunting me. I needed to see myself in a new light. I imagined that maybe I could get a few pinup model style photos. Those ladies were never stick thin. They had curves, attitude and unapologetic thighs, like me.

The photographer was awesome. I chose a female photographer because her business tagline spoke to me. "Look. Feel. BE. Beautiful!" I wanted that to be true for me.

It turned out to be an amazing choice, like the woman herself. She was no skinny mini. She was warm, encouraging, and her studio was a girls' dress-up closet. She had every type of beautiful frilly, girly thing you could imagine. It was over-the-top in the best possible way. Crowns and tiaras. Feathered fans. Fascinators in every color. A black lace veil that screamed drama. A hot pink parasol. Perfume bottles with poufy pumps. Powder puffs the size of dinner plates. Necklaces, earrings, gloves, boas. I wanted to wear it all and drape myself over her red velvet couch.

"I don't know what to do", I said, suddenly nervous when we were about to start and she stood over me with her camera.

"Don't worry," she said. "I got you. I don't look good, unless you look good. We'll start in your regular clothes and you can take off as much or as little as you want."

She coached me through every pose, every angle. She had some upbeat girly-pop music piped through the studio. In between shots and poses, we would both start singing along to Alicia Keys, Rihanna, Beyoncé. I felt like a "girl on fire", the "only girl in the world".

The photographer ooh-ed at the back of the camera like she'd shot a *Vogue* masterpiece.

"You have to see this shot," she said, flipping the screen toward me. There I was, a sexy fatty. That was me. I looked good. I looked *great*. I looked like someone I would want to flirt with. I wanted to ask me for my number.

Charlene whispered, *"Oh là là, Cherie, you're serving curves and confidence. You make that bikini look good."*

It was so fun, and in the midst of it all, I didn't even need to see the photos anymore. Just the experience of getting out of my head, feeling sexy and beautiful, that was all I needed.

"I'll work on your photos and send them to you in about two weeks," she said. "You can select your book and prints from the link I'll send you online. You were an awesome model, so beautiful and fun. I love your red bikini."

So do I.

**Charlene**: *"Red bikini. Full confidence. Zero apologies. I say we are ready for poolside martinis."*

# Eleven

## WE ALL HAVE BODY PAINS



Is this the end of us?

The Dude just blew up at me. He came home with four boxes of Indian food for us – four boxes! I know I said I love when he brings food for me, but I think this was excessive. So, I asked him outright.

"Why are you always doing this? You complain that I'm chunky, and then you try to stuff me with food. You're undermining all my healthy efforts. Are you deliberately trying to sabotage me?"

He looked like I had drawn a gun on him.

"I can't do anything right with you or for you. I didn't say anything when you lost your mind over a bikini party or when Tanya cried all over you at the wedding because she was jealous. I didn't tell you not to bother about the silly clothes lady who made you feel frumpy. I have been trying to be supportive, quietly having your back," he said.

He kept going. "You complained about getting fat. I was only agreeing when you said it. You decided you didn't want to go to the gym, then you went for two months of personal training. You complained about it the whole time: the classes, the mirrors, the gym wear, the trainer. I was trying to help you by ordering the gym equipment and workout tapes for you. Okay, so I used your card, not mine. But it was all for you. There would be no guys harassing you, no passive aggressive mirrors. Neither you nor me would have to hear all Chad's stupid opinions."

"I should have gotten a medal for putting up with 'Chad said' for three months. You've tried to change me, change us, dragging me into adventure trips. I don't want that. I just want you to be the woman I have always loved.

"If your girlfriends aren't happy, why come home and argue with me about what their boyfriends did or didn't do? *I* wasn't the cheater or the shallow one or the jerk. Why am I the one that always get the blame?

"You even said you were going to look for a muscle man to save you. How am I supposed to feel about that while you run off to the gym every other day?

"I've been bringing you food for months. We have always been cooking together and doing foodie trips. Suddenly, everything I do is wrong, and all I've ever done is not enough for you. Am I the enemy because I care and I want you to be happy? With Charlene, without Charlene, it doesn't matter if you aren't happy. You are the one complaining, obsessing, really. I haven't stopped loving you."

My usually mild-mannered boyfriend just had a full-on rant with me for five minutes, and now he's gone. Had he been nursing these thoughts all these months? He barely speaks and just mumbles when I ask him direct questions and this, this is the straw that breaks us. What in the world?

I've always expected him to be here, listening to me rant and letting me cuddle up on him when I let it all out. I didn't mean to make him feel unappreciated. I don't want to change him at all. I love him, just as he is, with Charlie too.

Maybe I've been too obsessive over Charlene. Maybe I really am as self-absorbed and dominating as Lucy has suggested. He has been so sweet and apologetic over the credit card thing. He did come along to the gym a few times and supported all my attempts at self-improvement.

There's so much great about him that I haven't written here. I just knew he'd be with me, like Charlene has been with me. Could we be over just like that, over one little comment? I can't believe it.

**Charlene***: "Girl, breathe. Maybe this had to happen. He's been taking you for granted, and the two of you really need to talk. Also, ice cream may help now."*

Monday, September 3, 2018

The Dude did not come back to my place after he left yesterday. I didn't have any appetite to eat, so I threw out three boxes of Indian food. I threw away *food*. That's how I know I'm not okay.

I feel awful. His words keep replaying in my head, each one sharper than the last. How awful I have been. How completely self-absorbed. How blind to the fact that the people around me have their own battles, too. I've been judgmental, catty, wrapped up in my own insecurities, while he has been understanding and patient. How do I make it up to him?

It's so serious that cake or ice cream doesn't feel like a solution. I think we need to take food out of the equation entirely. We have based too much of our relationship around our unhealthy coping with food. That I'm actually thinking this is also saying something. I have started thinking differently on how I approach food, exercise, and my body.

I have all this nervous energy. Maybe I'll finally throw the clothes off the bike he bought me and use it. I can sweat out some of my guilt and come up with a new plan for us.

I don't know what else to say.

On the plus side, I got my photos back from the photographer today. I love them, all of them. Even the ones with Charlene front and center, unapologetically taking up the frame. My first thought was to call The Dude, to share them with him. I wanted him to see how beautiful I looked, for him to agree that I was beautiful. Then I stopped. No, this shoot was for me, not for him.

I've been chasing external validation all along, in diets, in clothes shopping, in the gym, in his approval. But looking at those photos, I felt it for myself. For the first time, I saw me. Not the flaws, not the insecurities, but the woman who dared to pose, to play, to own her body. The photos spoke more loudly than any compliment he could have given. I wouldn't have believed him anyway.

Charlene whispered, *"See? You don't need him to tell you. You needed to see yourself."*

I still have to figure out what we need to say to each other to fix our rift. Or maybe I need to figure out if fixing it is even the right thing.

**Charlene**: *"Just saying, maybe ice cream and cake can be part of a solution. Try a little and see."*

I went down to maintenance today with a box of chocolate donuts for The Dude and his crew. It was a peace offering and also a decoy to get the guys off our backs so we could talk. It had been a long time since I'd come looking for him in our building. First time I'd ever brought him food at the office. He'd always been the one taking care of me: snacks, errands, his practical little gestures of care. Today I wanted to take care of him.

"Are we over? Are you still mad at me?" I asked, my voice smaller than I wanted it to be.

He wasn't mad. "We're not over. We needed a few days to clear the air," he said.

"Are you sure? It seemed pretty harsh. Pretty final."

"I was upset. You've been so different. Obsessed with Charlene, the gym, everything else. I wondered if you weren't into me anymore. I want us to be the team we used to be," he said.

"I want us to be a team too," I said.

"I'll never say no to your cake, either, if you are baking. I'll come see you later." I kissed him right there in front of his team. Another first, because neither of us have been big on public displays. The maintenance guys started hooting at us, like schoolboys. I didn't care. I needed him to know that he's all I want.

He surprised me again. "Don't you still have that company thing this weekend? Do you want me to come with you?" He even asked about the dress code for my company awards event on Saturday. He had remembered and even arranged to rent a dress suit already.

I was delighted. He still wanted to show up for me. He still wanted to be part of my world.

I think we will be okay. I hope we will be okay.

**Charlene**: *"Girl, showing up is half the battle. Talking is the next part. You'll be okay. I'm right here with you. Where's my donut?"*

Charlene and I still can't say no to carrot cake muffins.

I saw Bella today at my usual coffee spot and she wasn't alone. Her companion was a swarthy guy. I'm trying to find a nicer way to say not skinny, not muscley, but more barreled than The Dude. She waved me over and introduced me to her friend. Apparently, he works in a sneaker shop and had been giving her advice on the best running shoes. He runs too, and he's volunteered to be security for the ladies' running club. It's a good sign when there is genuine care and concern. I hope this relationship, if that's where it's headed, works out for her.

I'm still so impressed at how committed Bella is to her fitness, even though she appears outside the BMI ranges. The social cost of her larger size is probably the most difficult part of her journey. So few people are willing to see beyond the surface. Plus, dumb dudes with fat fetishes can trick women into worse circumstances. I am in the trenches with her when it comes to the reality of emotional eating and comfort food. I'm glad that she has found her crew of fitness warriors, and a seemingly stable man at her side, too.

**Charlene:** *"Go Bella, go Charlene. Bellies for the win."*

*Sunday, September 9 2018*

I want to say that I saw it coming, but I didn't.

Marcus and Tanya are an unlikely couple in the making. Last night was the Founders' gala, our big company recognition event. It was a swanky black-tie shindig. I ordered a fabulous one-shoulder orange sequined dress (online again, but from Bella's favorite boutiques) and I was delighted it fit as expected. Charlene and I, and The Dude, looked amazing.

When Marcus made his entrance with Tanya along as his plus-one, I had to hide my surprise and not drop my champagne. The sly dog never hinted that he was doing more than helping with her "Fitstagram". Sure, I'd spotted him in a couple of her posts, but didn't think much of it. He isn't more muscled, and his legs are still skinny despite all the high-intensity workouts. He swears by CrossFit now as the key to it all.

Maybe Tanya dropped a dumbbell on his toe, because he doesn't crack any more fat jokes around me. In fact, he's defensive when the other guys say dumb shit about women. Maybe he has learned a thing or two from interacting with real living women, instead of his "buds".

Truly, he and Tanya looked happy. She complimented me on my gown. It really was very flattering. The Dude had even matched his tie to my dress, and she said we look perfectly matched. I told her that she made Marcus look good. She laughed, agreed and added that he cleaned up well. I think this one has legs.

Tanya is still focused on her body journey. She has become the poster girl for workout and body definition, channeling her fitness passion into her influencer era. I couldn't do it with her because she goes way hard. Still, I understand her motivation.

When we talk now, she's been considerate of me and Charlene lately, even though I don't join her sweat sessions. Some of her online fans echoed my words to her, reminding her that people of all sizes struggle with body issues. She realized that my acceptance and naming of Charlene was part of my journey to body acceptance. Our flaws are not isolated body parts. They magnify our self-image. As a mentor now, she starts with encouraging patient self-love and determination to be healthy, rather than chasing a specific body shape.

She even joked that the idea of Charlene has taught her a thing or two about body love. Charlene piped up, *"See? I'm not just belly fat, I'm your curriculum. If you listen to me, you'll be more confident and well-fed, too."*

We do need to embrace our personal challenges and figure out what lessons they are bringing to our attention. Charlene is an intimate mentor, representing my personal insecurities. Maybe she's teaching Tanya too, to listen to her body as well.

**Charlene**: *"Tanya is finally seeing the light. Hooray!"*

*Monday, September 10, 2018*

The Dude surprised me this morning by staying over, and getting up to cook me breakfast. I watched him, confused.

"Why are you here cooking for me now?" I asked.

"I know after hanging with Tanya, you usually shut down. I don't want you to spiraling back into a bad place, like with the bikini party. I want to make sure you're okay." He looked at me closely, like he was trying to read my pulse with his eyes.

"I'm good, actually. Really good." I assured him, and I meant it. Saturday night, seeing Tanya in her figure-hugging red dress, I didn't feel any less than her. I was proud of my hot friend, happy that she was happy. I know she has her own struggles. Charlene and I aren't in competition with her. We never have been and I think she knows that too.

"I know I haven't always given you credit for how you've supported me. But we can't always be making up over food. There has to be a way for us to connect without carb-loading. I'm trying to make more intentional choices about my health and I want you there with me. I'm not trying to change you either; I want us to both be healthy and happy," I said.

He hesitated, then said, "I don't want you to try to 'glow up' and then decide I'm not the one for you, because you want a muscle hero. I could probably lift you, you know. I'm sorry if I ever made you feel like you are too much. You're my girl. I love you and want to take care of you. Part of that is feeding you, making sure you are satisfied."

"I appreciate that and I appreciate you," I said.

Charlene whispered, *"Girl, bacon is his love language. Don't fight it. Just insist that he appreciates the masterpiece his cooking is helping to craft."*

The Dude was as insightful as ever. Now he was saying out loud what I needed to hear. We both needed reassurance, and here it was in words and deeds. Who could argue with that, and bacon too?

Still, I know he has his own body image issues. He is hung up on the muscleman ideal, even though he doesn't seem to be working toward it. Just when I got out of my gym subscription, The Dude subscribed to *Men's Fitness* magazine. He is not oblivious to the men's version of the programming those magazines push. The protein shakes, health muffins, cardboard superfoods, green goop macro boosters, and diet pills all feed into our collective insecurity. It's a grab for our wallets through our body pains. Their sales pitch is about macros and protein shakes, the perfect set of weights and which sneakers will help you train harder. The goal is endless reps and sculpted abs. Reading this while stretched out on the couch reinforces personal insecurities. His body goals are just dreams.

The Dude is not alone. If I'm being fair, all guys have their insecurities, from hairlines to junk size, skipped leg days, man boobs and beer bellies. Men get a pass to be a little lumpier and even the dad bod is celebrated. Why can't the mom bod get the same respect? Why do women have to "bounce back"? What if you never had the hot body to start with? Where does my bountiful Charlene belly fit into the plan?

**Charlene**: *"Girl, we're the whole plan. It's not that we're too big, their imagination is too small. We don't have to fit into their mold. We have to make our own."*

*Saturday, September 15, 2018*

It finally happened. I wore my red flirty bikini.

There was a community barbecue poolside and I decided this is the moment. It is time for your girl to shine. That red bikini couldn't mock me anymore. I had already seen myself in its full glory. Now it was time to show everyone else that I wasn't afraid. Charlene and I were ready for our grand reveal.

Don't get carried away. Let me remind you, this was no itsy-bitsy bikini. This was a full-coverage, high-waisted ruffled brief and only my navel could peek out. The girls were adequately supported in the halter style wire bra with lovely crisscross straps and off-the-shoulder ruffles as well. Think of a glamorous pinup model. Have you noticed the full-coverage boy shorts style swimwear in those vintage photos? That's my kind of sexy, flattering and still leaving something to the imagination.

When I checked myself in the bathroom mirror, it didn't whisper any horror stories. It was on board with my look. My internal mirror voice gave me encouragement. Charlene smirked, "*Girl, you are serving Venus realness. Botticelli would've painted you twice. Now we should go do another boudoir shoot and take it all off. The Renaissance artists painted nudes and I would be a source of inspiration au naturelle.*"

That's how I felt, like a Renaissance muse. My female curves should be celebrated like in those portraits of the masters. Botticelli and Raphael immortalized women's figures that in today's magazines would be airbrushed away. I looked at my reflection and decided I liked my softness and my curves. Today I would embody Botticelli's Venus and not shy away from the body that I have.

Yes, I walked out the door in a brightly colored kimono. I'm not bold enough to strut through the apartment complex halls in only a bikini. I have lost a couple pounds, not my mind. But when I got to the pool, I slipped off said kimono to get into the water. Nothing imploded. Nothing exploded. No one had a bad word to say.

The Dude told me I looked beautiful and he was glad that I was there with him.

This was my non-scale victory. Bring on the bikinis and martinis. I am ready now.

**Charlene:** "*We looked good. You don't have to tell me twice, and the barbecue was delicious.*"

*Sunday, September 16, 2018*

Charlene and I, we are mostly cool these days. I'm starting to get this self-love thing. Sure, I'm still judgy and insecure some days, but I am giving myself, and others around me, a little grace.

I'm not obsessive over workouts or diets anymore. Instead, I'm taking the stairs, generally moving more and making better food choices. Calm acceptance paired with healthy goals is the path I'm on. The real change has been internal. The shift has been mental.

Charlene is not a problem to be solved. Dimples and muffin tops be damned. She's my diary of food choices, my metabolism, and maybe a few too many cheat meals and dreamy desserts. She's also as good to me as I am to her. In treating myself better with more activity and less emotional eating, she seems to be less bothersome.

I'm keeping up the fiber and drinking gallons of water, and wearing clothes that fit. No Spanx torture chambers, no oversized jackets to hide behind. I'm wearing comfortable, polished outfits. The mirror doesn't feel like my enemy. It is only a reflection. The surprising thing is that I look at other women less critically, because I see myself in them.

Besides, all my girlfriends were struggling with the same thing in different ways. Everyone has their personal bête noire.

Even Lucy, who seemed immune to body issues, got uncomfortable when she was complimented. Something triggered her, too. There's always the subtle whisper of competition for the perfect body, or face, or style. I still can't believe she was taken in by Greg.

No one I know is perfectly content. Slim, fat, or average, it doesn't matter. There is a whole conspiracy industry out there: gyms selling impossible contracts, cosmetics promising to stop time, fashion magazines promoting styles that fit no one, plastic surgery offering dangerous shortcuts. Their tentacles are everywhere, extracting self-esteem by any means necessary.

I'm done demoralizing myself with magazines. Here is my new body affirmation: My jelly belly is a sexy French maid with a built-in apron!!!

The truth is, no one thinks they have the perfect body. You have the body you've got, and you've got to treat it right. Neither sex has a monopoly on body issues, though men seem to get more of a pass.

I still have weight to lose but I am going to live with this body. It's the one I am going to die with, fat or slim.

After all, I named my belly fat Charlene, and I think I like her.

**Charlene**: *"Of course you love me, I'm fabulous, Cherie!"*

# About the Author

Louanne McFarlane is a science professional for her day job, and a creative with every other aspect of her life. She writes with wit, warmth, and a keen eye for the everyday absurdities of life.

When not drafting stories, Louanne enjoys photography, reading, and hanging out with family and friends. Her debut novel, *I Named My Belly Fat Charlene,* blends humor and honesty in a diary-style exploration of self-acceptance, proving that even our quirks deserve a spotlight.

Meet her here:

https://www.facebook.com/charlenebellyfat or visit www.charlenebellyfat.com